LEILA

LEILA

SIR EDWARD BULWER-LYTTON

WILDSIDE PRESS

Published by Wildside Press LLC.
www.wildsidebooks.com

TO

THE COUNTESS OF BLESSINGTON

𝕿𝖍𝖎𝖘 𝕿𝖆𝖑𝖊 𝖎𝖘 𝕯𝖊𝖉𝖎𝖈𝖆𝖙𝖊𝖉,

BY ONE

WHO WISHES HE COULD HAVE FOUND A MORE DURABLE MONUMENT
WHEREON TO ENGRAVE

A MEMORIAL OF REAL FRIENDSHIP.

CONTENTS.

LEILA; OR, THE SIEGE OF GRANADA.

Book I.

Book II.

Book III.

𝕭ook IV.

𝕭ook V.

CONTENTS.

LEILA;

OR,

THE SIEGE OF GRANADA.

⸻◆⸻

BOOK I.

―――

CHAPTER I.

THE ENCHANTER AND THE WARRIOR.

It was the summer of the year 1491, and the armies of
Ferdinand and Isabel invested the city of Granada.

The night was not far advanced; and the moon, which
broke through the transparent air of Andalusia, shone calmly
over the immense and murmuring encampment of the Spanish
foe, and touched with a hazy light the snow-capped summits
of the Sierra Nevada, contrasting the verdure and luxuriance
which no devastation of man could utterly sweep from the
beautiful vale below.

In the streets of the Moorish city many a group still lingered. Some, as if unconscious of the beleaguering war
without, were listening in quiet indolence to the strings of
the Moorish lute or the lively tale of an Arabian improvisa-
tor; others were conversing with such eager and animated
gestures as no ordinary excitement could wring from the
stately calm habitual to every Oriental people. But the
more public places, in which gathered these different groups,
only the more impressively heightened the desolate and solemn repose that brooded over the rest of the city.

At this time a man, with downcast eyes, and arms folded
within the sweeping gown which descended to his feet, was

seen passing through the streets, alone, and apparently unobservant of all around him. Yet this indifference was by no means shared by the struggling crowds through which, from time to time, he musingly swept.

"God is great!" said one man; "it is the Enchanter Almamen."

"He hath locked up the manhood of Boabdil el Chico with the key of his spells," quoth another, stroking his beard; "I would curse him, if I dared."

"But they say that he hath promised that when man fails, the genii will fight for Granada," observed a third, doubtingly.

"Allah Akbar! what is, is; what shall be, shall be!" said a fourth, with all the solemn sagacity of a prophet.

Whatever their feelings, whether of awe or execration, terror or hope, each group gave way as Almamen passed, and hushed the murmurs not intended for his ear. Passing through the Zacatin (the street which traversed the Great Bazaar), the reputed enchanter ascended a narrow and winding street, and arrived at last before the walls that encircled the palace and fortress of the Alhambra.

The sentry at the gate saluted and admitted him in silence; and in a few moments his form was lost in the solitude of groves, amidst which at frequent openings the spray of Arabian fountains glittered in the moonlight; while above rose the castled heights of the Alhambra; and on the right, those Vermilion Towers whose origin veils itself in the farthest ages of Phœnician enterprise.

Almamen paused, and surveyed the scene. "Was Aden more lovely?" he muttered; "and shall so fair a spot be trodden by the victor Nazarene? What matters? Creed chases creed, race, race, until time comes back to its starting-place, and beholds the reign restored to the eldest faith and the eldest tribe. The horn of our strength shall be exalted."

At these thoughts the seer relapsed into silence, and gazed long and intently upon the stars, as, more numerous and brilliant with every step of the advancing night, their rays broke on the playful waters, and tinged with silver the various and breathless foliage. So earnest was his gaze, and so absorbed his thoughts, that he did not perceive the approach of a Moor, whose glittering weapons and snow-white turban, rich with emeralds, cast a gleam through the wood.

The new-comer was above the common size of his race, — generally small and spare, — but without attaining the lofty stature and large proportions of the more redoubted of the warriors of Spain. But in his presence and mien there was something which, in the haughtiest conclave of Christian chivalry, would have seemed to tower and command. He walked with a step at once light and stately, as if it spurned the earth; and in the carriage of the small erect head and stag-like throat there was that indefinable and imposing dignity which accords so well with our conception of a heroic lineage and a noble though imperious spirit. The stranger approached Almamen, and paused abruptly when within a few steps of the enchanter. He gazed upon him in silence for some moments; and when at length he spoke, it was with a cold and sarcastic tone.

"Pretender to the dark secrets," said he, "is it in the stars that thou art reading those destinies of men and nations which the Prophet wrought by the chieftain's brain and the soldier's arm?"

"Prince," replied Almamen, turning slowly, and recognizing the intruder on his meditations, "I was but considering how many revolutions, which have shaken earth to its centre, those orbs have witnessed, unsympathizing and unchanged."

"Unsympathizing!" repeated the Moor, — "yet thou believest in their effect upon the earth?"

"You wrong me," answered Almamen, with a slight smile; "you confound your servant with that vain race, the astrologers."

"I deemed astrology a part of the science of the two angels, Harût and Marût."[1]

"Possibly; but I know not that science, though I have 'wandered at midnight by the ancient Babel."

---

[1] The science of magic. It was taught by the angels named in the text; for which offence they are still supposed to be confined to the ancient Babel. There they may yet be consulted, though they are rarely seen (*Yallal' odin Yahya*). — SALE: *Koran.*

"Fame lies to us, then," answered the Moor, with some surprise.

"Fame never made pretence to truth," said Almamen, calmly, and proceeding on his way. "Allah be with you, prince; I seek the king."

"Stay! I have just quitted his presence, and left him, I trust, with thoughts worthy of the sovereign of Granada, which I would not have disturbed by a stranger, a man whose arms are not spear nor shield."

"Noble Muza," returned Almamen, "fear not that my voice will weaken the inspirations which thine hath breathed into the breast of Boabdil. Alas! if my counsel were heeded, thou wouldst hear the warriors of Granada talk less of Muza, and more of the king. But Fate, or Allah, hath placed upon the throne of a tottering dynasty one who, though brave, is weak, though wise, a dreamer; and you suspect the adviser when you find the influence of nature on the advised. Is this just?"

Muza gazed long and sternly on the face of Almamen; then, putting his hand gently on the enchanter's shoulder, he said, —

"Stranger, if thou playest us false, think that this arm hath cloven the casque of many a foe, and will not spare the turban of a traitor!"

"And think thou, proud prince," returned Almamen, unquailing, "that I answer alone to Allah for my motives, and that against man my deeds I can defend!"

With these words the enchanter drew his long robe round him, and disappeared amidst the foliage.

CHAPTER II.

THE KING WITHIN HIS PALACE.

In one of those apartments, the luxury of which is known only to the inhabitants of a genial climate (half chamber and half grotto), reclined a young Moor, in a thoughtful and musing attitude.

The ceiling of cedar-wood, glowing with gold and azure, was supported by slender shafts of the whitest alabaster, between which were open arcades light and graceful as the arched vineyards of Italy, and wrought in that delicate filigree-work common to the Arabian architecture; through these arcades was seen at intervals the lapsing fall of waters, lighted by alabaster lamps, and their tinkling music sounded with a fresh and regular murmur upon the ear. The whole of one side of this apartment was open to a broad and extensive balcony, which overhung the banks of the winding and moonlit Darro; and in the clearness of the soft night might be distinctly seen the undulating hills, the woods and orange-groves, which still form the unrivalled landscapes of Granada.

The pavement was spread with ottomans and couches of the richest azure, prodigally enriched with quaint designs in broideries of gold and silver; and over that on which the Moor reclined, facing the open balcony, were suspended on a pillar the round shield, the light javelin, and the curving cimeter of Moorish warfare. So studded were these arms with jewels of rare cost that they might alone have sufficed to indicate the rank of the evident owner, even if his own gorgeous vestments had not betrayed it. An open manuscript on a silver table lay unread before the Moor as, leaning his face upon his hand, he looked with abstracted eyes along the mountain summits dimly distinguished from the cloudless and far horizon.

No one could have gazed without a vague emotion of interest, mixed with melancholy, upon the countenance of the inmate of that luxurious chamber.

Its beauty was singularly stamped with a grave and stately sadness, which was made still more impressive by its air of youth and the unwonted fairness of the complexion. Unlike the attributes of the Moorish race, the hair and curling beard were of a deep golden colour; and on the broad forehead and in the large eyes was that settled and contemplative mildness which rarely softens the swart lineaments of the fiery children of the sun. Such was the personal appearance of Boabdil el Chico, the last of the Moorish dynasty in Spain.

"These scrolls of Arabian learning," said Boabdil to himself, "what do they teach? To despise wealth and power, to hold the heart to be the true empire. This, then, is wisdom. Yet if I follow these maxims am I wise? Alas! the whole world would call me a driveller and a madman. Thus is it ever; the wisdom of the Intellect fills us with precepts which it is the wisdom of Action to despise. O Holy Prophet, what fools men would be, if their knavery did not eclipse their folly!"

The young king listlessly threw himself back on his cushions as he uttered these words, too philosophical for a king whose crown sat so loosely on his brow.

After a few moments of thought that appeared to dissatisfy and disquiet him, Boabdil again turned impatiently round. "My soul wants the bath of music," said he; "these journeys into a pathless realm have wearied it, and the streams of sound supple and relax the travailed pilgrim."

He clapped his hands, and from one of the arcades a boy, hitherto invisible, started into sight; at a slight and scarce perceptible sign from the king the boy again vanished, and in a few moments afterwards, glancing through the fairy pillars and by the glittering waterfalls, came the small and twinkling feet of the maids of Araby. As with their transparent tunics and white arms they gleamed, without an echo, through that cool and voluptuous chamber, they might well have seemed the Peris of the Eastern magic, summoned to beguile the sated leisure of a youthful Solomon. With them came a maiden of more exquisite beauty, though smaller stature, than the rest, bearing the light Moorish lute; and a faint and languid smile broke over the beautiful face of Boabdil as his eyes rested upon her graceful form and the dark yet glowing lustre of her Oriental countenance. She alone approached the king, timidly kissed his hand, and then, joining her comrades, commenced the following song, to the air and very words of which the feet of the dancing-girls kept time, while with the chorus rang the silver bells of the musical instrument which each of the dancers carried.

AMINE'S SONG.

I.

Softly, oh, softly glide,
Gentle Music, thou silver tide,
Bearing, the lulled air along,
This leaf from the Rose of Song!
　　To its port in his soul let it float,
　　The frail but the fragrant boat, —
　　　Bear it, soft Air, along!

II.

With the burthen of sound we are laden,
Like the bells on the trees of Aden,[1]
When they thrill with a tinkling tone
At the Wind from the Holy Throne.
　　Hark, as we move around,
　　We shake off the buds of sound:
　　　Thy presence, Belovéd, is Aden.

III.

Sweet chime that I hear and wake,
I would, for my loved one's sake,
That I were a sound like thee,
To the depths of his heart to flee.
　　If my breath had his senses blest,
　　If my voice in his heart could rest,
　　　What pleasure to die like thee!

---

[1] The Mohammedans believe that musical bells hang on the trees of Paradise, and are put in motion by a wind from the throne of God.

The music ceased; the dancers remained motionless in their graceful postures, as if arrested into statues of alabaster; and the young songstress cast herself on a cushion at the feet of the monarch, and looked up fondly, but silently, into his yet melancholy eyes, when a man, whose entrance had not been noticed, was seen to stand within the chamber.

He was about the middle stature, lean, muscular, and strongly though sparely built. A plain black robe, something in the fashion of the Armenian gown, hung long and loosely over a tunic of bright scarlet, girded by a broad belt, from the centre of which was suspended a small golden key, while at the left side appeared the jewelled hilt of a crooked dagger. His features were cast in a larger and grander mould than was common among the Moors of Spain: the forehead was broad, massive, and singularly high, and the dark eyes were of unusual size and brilliancy; his beard, short, black, and glossy, curled upward, and concealed all the lower part of the face, save a firm, compressed, and resolute expression in the lips, which were large and full; the nose was high, aquiline, and well-shaped; and the whole character of the head (which was, for symmetry, on too large and gigantic a scale as proportioned to the form) was indicative of extraordinary energy and power. At the first glance, the stranger might have seemed scarce on the borders of middle age; but on a more careful examination, the deep lines and wrinkles, marked on the forehead and round the eyes, betrayed a more advanced period of life. With arms folded on his breast, he stood by the side of the king, waiting in silence the moment when his presence should be perceived.

He did not wait long; the eyes and gesture of the girl nestled at the feet of Boabdil drew the king's attention to the spot where the stranger stood. His eye brightened when it fell upon him.

"Almamen," cried Boabdil, eagerly, "you are welcome." As he spoke, he motioned to the dancing-girls to withdraw.

"May I not rest? O core of my heart, thy bird is in its home," murmured the songstress at the king's feet.

"Sweet Amine," answered Boabdil, tenderly smoothing

down her ringlets as he bent to kiss her brow, "you should witness only my hours of delight. Toil and business have nought with thee; I will join thee ere yet the nightingale hymns his last music to the moon." Amine sighed, rose, and vanished with her companions.

"My friend," said the king, when alone with Almamen, "your counsels often soothe me into quiet, yet in such hours quiet is a crime. But what do? How struggle, — how act? Alas! at the hour of his birth, rightly did they affix to the name of Boabdil the epithet of *El Zogoybi*.[1] Misfortune set upon my brow her dark and fated stamp ere yet my lips could shape a prayer against her power. My fierce father, whose frown was as the frown of Azrael, hated me in my cradle; in my youth my name was invoked by rebels against my will; imprisoned by my father, with the poison-bowl or the dagger hourly before my eyes, I was saved only by the artifice of my mother. When age and infirmity broke the iron sceptre of the king, my claims to the throne were set aside, and my uncle, El Zagal, usurped my birthright. Amidst open war and secret treason I wrestled for my crown; and now, the sole sovereign of Granada, when, as I fondly imagined, my uncle had lost all claim on the affections of my people by succumbing to the Christian king and accepting a fief under his dominion, I find that the very crime of El Zagal is fixed upon me by my unhappy subjects, — that they deem he would not have yielded but for my supineness. At the moment of my delivery from my rival, I am received with execration by my subjects, and, driven into this my fortress of the Alhambra, dare not venture to head my armies or to face my people; yet am I called weak and irresolute, when strength and courage are forbid me. And as the water glides from yonder rock, that hath no power to retain it, I see the tide of empire welling from my hands."

The young king spoke warmly and bitterly, and in the irritation of his thoughts strode, while he spoke, with rapid and irregular strides along the chamber. Almamen marked his emotion with an eye and a lip of rigid composure.

---

[1] The unlucky.

"Light of the faithful," said he, when Boabdil had con-cluded, "the powers above never doom man to perpetual sor-row nor perpetual joy. The cloud and the sunshine are alike essential to the heaven of our destinies; and if thou hast suf-fered in thy youth, thou hast exhausted the calamities of fate, and thy manhood will be glorious, and thine age serene."

"Thou speakest as if the armies of Ferdinand were not already around my walls," said Boabdil, impatiently.

"The armies of Sennacherib were as mighty," answered Almamen.

"Wise seer," returned the king, in a tone half sarcastic and half solemn, "we, the Mussulmans of Spain, are not the blind fanatics of the Eastern world. On us have fallen the lights of philosophy and science; and if the more clear-sighted among us yet outwardly reverence the forms and fables worshipped by the multitude, it is from the wisdom of policy, not the folly of belief. Talk not to me, then, of thine examples of the ancient and elder creeds; the agents of God for this world are now, at least, in men, not angels; and if I wait till Ferdinand share the destiny of Sennacherib, I wait only till the Standard of the Cross wave above the Vermilion Towers."

"Yet," said Almamen, "while my lord the king rejects the fanaticism of belief, doth he reject the fanaticism of persecu-tion? You disbelieve the stories of the Hebrews, yet you suffer the Hebrews themselves, that ancient and kindred Arabian race, to be ground to the dust, condemned and tor-tured by your judges, your informers, your soldiers, and your subjects."

"The base misers, they deserve their fate," answered Boabdil, loftily. "Gold is their god, and the market-place their country. Amidst the tears and groans of nations, they sympathize only with the rise and fall of trade; and, the thieves of the universe, while their hand is against every man's coffer, why wonder that they provoke the hand of every man against their throats? Worse than the tribe of Hanifa, who eat their god only in time of famine,[1] the race

[1] The tribe of Hanifa worshipped a lump of dough.

of Moisa[1] would sell the Seven Heavens for the dent[2] on the back of the date-stone."

"Your laws leave them no ambition but that of avarice," replied Almamen; "and as the plant will crook and distort its trunk, to raise its head through every obstacle to the sun, so the mind of man twists and perverts itself, if legitimate openings are denied it, to find its natural element in the gale of power or the sunshine of esteem. These Hebrews were not traffickers and misers in their own sacred land when they routed your ancestors, the Arab armies of old, and gnawed the flesh from their bones in famine rather than yield a weaker city than Granada to a mightier force than the holiday lords of Spain. Let this pass. My lord rejects the belief in the agencies of the angels; doth he still retain belief in the wisdom of mortal men?"

"Yes," returned Boabdil, quickly; "for of the one I know nought; of the other, mine own senses can be the judge. Almamen, my fiery kinsman, Muza, hath this evening been with me. He hath urged me to reject the fears of my people, which chain my panting spirit within these walls; he hath urged me to gird on yonder shield and cimeter, and to appear in the Vivarrambla, at the head of the nobles of Granada. My heart leaps high at the thought; and if I cannot live, at least I will die — a king!"

"It is nobly spoken," said Almamen, coldly.

"You approve, then, my design?"

"The friends of the king cannot approve the ambition of the king to die."

"Ha!" said Boabdil, in an altered voice, "thou thinkest, then, that I am doomed to perish in this struggle?"

"As the hour shall be chosen, wilt thou fall or triumph."

"And that hour?"

"Is not yet come."

"Dost thou read the hour in the stars?"

"Let Moorish seers cultivate that frantic credulity; thy servant sees but in the stars worlds mightier than this little

---

[1] Moisa, Moses.

[2] A proverb used in the Koran, signifying the smallest possible trifle.

earth, whose light would neither wane nor wink if earth itself were swept from the infinities of space."

"Mysterious man," said Boabdil, "whence, then, is thy power? Whence thy knowledge of the future?"

Almamen approached the king, as he now stood by the open balcony.

"Behold," said he, pointing to the waters of the Darro, "yonder stream is of an element in which man cannot live nor breathe. Above, in the thin and impalpable air, our steps cannot find a footing, the armies of all earth cannot build an empire. And yet, by the exercise of a little art, the fishes and the birds, the inhabitants of the air and the water, minister to our most humble wants, the most common of our enjoyments. So it is with the true science of enchantment. Thinkest thou that, while the petty surface of the world is crowded with living things, there is no life in the vast centre within the earth, and the immense ether that surrounds it? As the fisherman snares his prey, as the fowler entraps the bird, so, by the art and genius of our human mind, we may thrall and command the subtler beings of realms and elements which our material bodies cannot enter, our gross senses cannot survey. This, then, is my lore. Of other worlds know I nought; but of the things of this world, whether men, or, as your legends term them, ghouls and genii, I have learned something. To the future, I myself am blind; but I can invoke and conjure up those whose eyes are more piercing, whose natures are more gifted."

"Prove to me thy power," said Boabdil, awed less by the words than by the thrilling voice and the impressive aspect of the enchanter.

"Is not the king's will my law?" answered Almamen. "Be his will obeyed. To-morrow night I await thee."

"Where?"

Almamen paused a moment, and then whispered a sentence in the king's ear. Boabdil started, and turned pale.

"A fearful spot!"

"So is the Alhambra itself, great Boabdil, while Ferdinand is without the walls, and Muza within the city."

"Muza! Darest thou mistrust my bravest warrior?"

"What wise king will trust the idol of the king's army? Did Boabdil fall to-morrow, by a chance javelin, in the field, whom would the nobles and the warriors place upon his throne? Doth it require an enchanter's lore to whisper to thy heart the answer in the name of ' Muza '?"

"O wretched state! O miserable king!" exclaimed Boabdil, in a tone of great anguish. "I never had a father, — I have now no people; a little while, and I shall have no country. Am I never to have a friend?"

"A friend, — what king ever had?" returned Almamen, dryly.

"Away, man, away!" cried Boabdil, as the impatient spirit of his rank and race shot dangerous fire from his eyes; "your cold and bloodless wisdom freezes up all the veins of my manhood! Glory, confidence, human sympathy, and feeling, — your counsels annihilate them all. Leave me; I would be alone."

"We meet to-morrow at midnight, mighty Boabdil," said Almamen, with his usual unmoved and passionless tones. "May the king live forever!"

The king turned, but his monitor had already disappeared. He went as he came, — noiseless and sudden as a ghost.

CHAPTER III.

THE LOVERS.

When Muza parted from Almamen, he bent his steps towards the hill that rises opposite the ascent crowned with the towers of the Alhambra, the sides and summit of which eminence were tenanted by the luxurious population of the city. He selected the more private and secluded paths; and, half way up the hill, arrived at last before a low wall of considerable extent, which girded the gardens of some wealthier inhabitant of the city. He looked long and anxiously round.

All was solitary, nor was the stillness broken save as an occasional breeze from the snowy heights of the Sierra Nevada rustled the fragrant leaves of the citron and pomegranate, or as the silver tinkling of waterfalls chimed melodiously within the gardens. The Moor's heart beat high. A moment more, and he had scaled the wall, and found himself upon a greensward, variegated by the rich colours of many a sleeping flower, and shaded by groves and alleys of luxuriant foliage and golden fruits.

It was not long before he stood beside a house that seemed of a construction anterior to the Moorish dynasty. It was built over low cloisters formed by heavy and time-worn pillars, concealed for the most part by a profusion of roses and creeping shrubs; the lattices above the cloisters opened upon large gilded balconies, — the superaddition of Moriscan taste. In one only of the casements a lamp was visible; the rest of the mansion was dark, as if, save in that chamber, sleep kept watch over the inmates. It was to this window that the Moor stole; and after a moment's pause he murmured rather than sang, so low and whispered was his voice, the following simple verses, slightly varied from an old Arabian poet: —

SERENADE.

Light of my soul, arise, arise,
Thy sister lights are in the skies!
        We want thine eyes,
        Thy joyous eyes;
The Night is mourning for thine eyes!

The sacred verse is on my sword,
    But on my heart thy name;
The words on each alike adored,
    The truth of each the same.
The same, — alas! too well I feel
The heart is truer than the steel.

Light of my soul, upon me shine!
Night wakes her stars to envy mine.
        Those eyes of thine,
        Wild eyes of thine,
What stars are like those eyes of thine?

As he concluded, the lattice softly opened, and a female form appeared on the balcony.

"Ah, Leila!" said the Moor, "I see thee, and I am blessed!"

"Hush!" answered Leila, "speak low, nor tarry long; I fear that our interviews are suspected. And this," she added, in a trembling voice, "may perhaps be the last time we shall meet."

"Holy Prophet!" exclaimed Muza, passionately, "what do I hear? Why this mystery? Why cannot I learn thine origin, thy rank, thy parents? Think you, beautiful Leila, that Granada holds a house lofty enough to disdain the alliance with Muza Ben Abil Gazan? And oh," he added, sinking the haughty tones of his voice into accents of the softest tenderness, "if not too high to scorn me, what should war against our loves and our bridals? For worn equally on my heart were the flower of thy sweet self, whether the mountain top or the valley gave birth to the odour and the bloom."

"Alas!" answered Leila, weeping, "the mystery thou complainest of is as dark to myself as thee. How often have I told thee that I know nothing of my birth or childish fortunes, save a dim memory of a more distant and burning clime, where, amidst sands and wastes, springs the everlasting cedar, and the camel grazes on stunted herbage withering in the fiery air? Then it seemed to me that I had a mother: fond eyes looked on me, and soft songs hushed me into sleep."

"Thy mother's soul has passed into mine," said the Moor, tenderly.

Leila continued: "Borne hither, I passed from childhood into youth within these walls. Slaves minister to my slightest wish; and those who have seen both state and poverty, which I have not, tell me that treasures and splendour that might glad a monarch are prodigalized around me. But of ties and kindred know I little; my father, a stern and silent man, visits me but rarely, — sometimes months pass, and I see him not; but I feel he loves me. And till I knew thee, Muza, my brightest hours were in listening to the footsteps and flying to the arms of that solitary friend."

"Know you not his name?"

"Nor I, nor any one of the household, save perhaps Ximen, the chief of the slaves, — an old and withered man, whose very eye chills me into fear and silence."

"Strange," said the Moor, musingly. "Yet why think you our love is discovered, or can be thwarted?"

"Hush! Ximen sought me this day. 'Maiden,' said he, 'men's footsteps have been tracked within the gardens: if your sire know this, you will have looked your last on Granada. Learn,' he added, in a softer voice, as he saw me tremble, 'that permission were easier given to thee to wed the wild tiger than to mate with the loftiest noble of Morisca. Beware!' He spoke, and left me. Oh, Muza," she continued, passionately wringing her hands, "my heart sinks within me, and omen and doom rise dark before my sight!"

"By my father's head, these obstacles but fire my love; and I would scale to thy possession, though every step in the ladder were the corpses of a hundred foes!"

Scarcely had the fiery and high-souled Moor uttered his boast, than, from some unseen hand amidst the groves, a javelin whirred past him, and as the air it raised came sharp upon his cheek, half buried its quivering shaft in the trunk of a tree behind him.

"Fly, fly, and save thyself! O God, protect him!" cried Leila; and she vanished within the chamber.

The Moor did not wait the result of a deadlier aim; he turned, — yet, in the instinct of his fierce nature, not from, but against, the foe; his drawn cimeter in his hand, the half-suppressed cry of wrath trembling on his lips, he sprang forward in the direction whence the javelin had sped. With eyes accustomed to the ambuscades of Moorish warfare, he searched eagerly, yet warily, through the dark and sighing foliage. No sign of life met his gaze; and at length, grimly and reluctantly he retraced his steps and quitted the demesnes: but just as he had cleared the wall a voice — low, but sharp and shrill — came from the gardens.

"Thou art spared," it said, "but haply for a more miserable doom!"

HALL OF THE DIVANS, THE ALHAMBRA.

CHAPTER IV.

THE FATHER AND DAUGHTER.

THE chamber into which Leila retreated bore out the character she had given of the interior of her home. The fashion of its ornament and decoration was foreign to that adopted by the Moors of Granada; it had a more massive and, if we may use the term, *Egyptian* gorgeousness. The walls were covered with the stuffs of the East, stiff with gold, embroidered upon ground of the deepest purple; strange characters, apparently in some foreign tongue, were wrought in the tessellated cornices and on the heavy ceiling, which was supported by square pillars, round which were twisted serpents of gold and enamel, with eyes to which enormous emeralds gave a green and lifelike glare; various scrolls and musical instruments lay scattered upon marble tables, and a solitary lamp of burnished silver cast a dim and subdued light around the chamber. The effect of the whole, though splendid, was gloomy, strange, and oppressive, and rather suited to the thick and cave-like architecture which of old protected the inhabitants of Thebes and Memphis from the rays of the African sun, than to the transparent heaven and light pavilions of the graceful Orientals of Granada.

Leila stood within this chamber, pale and breathless, with her lips apart, her hands clasped, her very soul in her ears; nor was it possible to conceive a more perfect ideal of some delicate and brilliant Peri, captured in the palace of a hostile and gloomy Genius. Her form was of the lightest shape consistent with the roundness of womanly beauty, and there was something in it of that elastic and fawnlike grace which a sculptor seeks to embody in his dreams of a being more aërial than those of earth. Her luxuriant hair was dark indeed, but a purple and glossy hue redeemed it from that heaviness of shade too common in the tresses of the Asiatics; and her complexion, naturally pale, but clear and lustrous, would have been deemed fair even in the North. Her features, slightly aquiline, were formed in the rarest mould of symmetry, and her full rich lips disclosed teeth that might have shamed the pearl. But the chief charm of that exquisite countenance was in an expression of softness and purity and intellectual sentiment that seldom accompanies that cast of loveliness, and was wholly foreign to the voluptuous and dreamy languor of Moorish maidens. Leila had been educated, and the statue had received a soul.

After a few minutes of intense suspense, she again stole to the lattice, gently unclosed it, and looked forth. Far, through an opening amidst the trees, she descried for a single moment the erect and stately figure of her lover darkening the moonshine on the sward, as now, quitting his fruitless search, he turned his lingering gaze towards the lattice of his beloved. The thick and interlacing foliage quickly hid him from her eyes; but Leila had seen enough; she turned within, and said, as grateful tears trickled down her cheeks, and she sank on her knees upon the piled cushions of the chamber, "God of my fathers, I bless thee, — he is safe!"

"And yet," she added, as a painful thought crossed her, "how may I pray for him? We kneel not to the same divinity, and I have been taught to loathe and shudder at his creed. Alas! how will this end? Fatal was the hour when he first beheld me in yonder gardens; more fatal still the hour in which he crossed the barrier, and told Leila that she was beloved by the hero whose arm was the shelter, whose name is the blessing, of Granada. Ah me, ah me!"

The young maiden covered her face with her hands, and sank into a passionate revery, broken only by her sobs. Some time had passed in this undisturbed indulgence of her grief, when the arras was gently put aside, and a man of remarkable garb and mien advanced into the chamber, pausing as he beheld her dejected attitude, and gazing on her with a look in which pity and tenderness seemed to struggle against habitual severity and sternness.

"Leila," said the intruder.

Leila started, and a deep blush suffused her countenance; she dashed the tears from her eyes, and came forward with a vain attempt to smile.

"My father, welcome!"

The stranger seated himself on the cushions, and motioned Leila to his side.

"These tears are fresh upon thy cheek," said he, gravely; "they are the witness of thy race. Our daughters are born to weep, and our sons to groan; ashes are on the head of the mighty, and the Fountains of the Beautiful run with gall! Oh that we could but struggle, that we could but dare, that we could raise up our heads, and unite against the bondage of the evil-doer! It may not be; but one man shall avenge a nation!"

The dark face of Leila's father, well fitted to express powerful emotion, became terrible in its wrath and passion; his brow and lip worked convulsively. But the paroxysm was brief; and scarce could she shudder at its intensity ere it had subsided into calm.

"Enough of these thoughts, which thou, a woman and a child, art not formed to witness. Leila, thou hast been nurtured with tenderness, and schooled with care. Harsh and unloving may I have seemed to thee, but I would have shed the best drops of my heart to save thy young years from a single pang. Nay, listen to me silently. That thou mightest one day be worthy of thy race, and that thine hours might not pass in indolent and weary lassitude, thou hast been taught the lessons of a knowledge rarely given to thy sex. Not thine the lascivious arts of the Moorish maidens; not thine their harlot songs, and their dances of lewd delight; thy delicate limbs were but taught the attitude that Nature dedicates to the worship of a God, and the music of thy voice was tuned to the songs of thy fallen country, sad with the memory of her wrongs, animated with the names of her heroes, holy with the solemnity of her prayers. These scrolls and the lessons of our seers have imparted to thee such of our science and our history as may fit thy mind to aspire, and thy heart to feel for a sacred cause. Thou listenest to me, Leila?"

Perplexed and wondering, for never before had her father addressed her in such a strain, the maiden answered with an earnestness of manner that seemed to content the questioner; and he resumed, with an altered, hollow, solemn voice, —

"Then curse the persecutors. Daughter of the great Hebrew race, arise and curse the Moorish taskmaster and spoiler!"

As he spoke, the adjuror himself rose, lifting his right hand on high, while his left touched the shoulder of the maiden. But she, after gazing a moment in wild and terrified amazement upon his face, fell cowering at his knees, and clasping them imploringly, exclaimed in scarce articulate murmurs, —

"Oh, spare me, spare me!"

The Hebrew — for such he was — surveyed her, as she thus quailed at his feet, with a look of rage and scorn; his hand wandered to his poniard, he half unsheathed it, thrust it back with a muttered curse, and then, deliberately drawing it forth, cast it on the ground beside her.

"Degenerate girl," he said, in accents that vainly struggled for calm, "if thou hast admitted to thy heart one unworthy thought towards a Moorish infidel, dig deep and root it out, even with the knife, and to the death, — so wilt thou save this hand from that degrading task."

He drew himself hastily from her grasp, and left the unfortunate girl alone and senseless.

CHAPTER V.

AMBITION DISTORTED INTO VICE BY LAW.

On descending a broad flight of stairs from the apartment, the Hebrew encountered an old man habited in loose garments of silk and fur, upon whose withered and wrinkled face life seemed scarcely to struggle against the advance of death, so haggard, wan, and corpse-like was its aspect.

"Ximen," said the Israelite, "trusty and beloved servant, follow me to the cavern."

He did not tarry for an answer, but continued his way with rapid strides through various courts and alleys, till he came at length into a narrow, dark, and damp gallery, that seemed cut from the living rock. At its entrance was a strong grate, which gave way to the Hebrew's touch upon the spring, though the united strength of a hundred men could not have moved it from its hinge. Taking up a brazen lamp that burned in a niche within it, the Hebrew paused impatiently till the feeble steps of the old man reached the spot, and then, reclosing the grate, pursued his winding way for a considerable distance, till he stopped suddenly by a part of the rock which seemed in no respect different from the rest; and so artfully contrived and concealed was the door which he now opened, and so suddenly did it yield to his hand, that it appeared literally the effect of enchantment when the rock yawned, and discovered a circular cavern lighted with brazen lamps, and spread with hangings and cushions of thick furs. Upon rude and seemingly natural pillars of rock, various antique and rusty arms were suspended; in large niches were deposited scrolls, clasped and bound with iron; and a profusion of strange and uncouth instruments and machines (in which modern science might perhaps discover the tools of chemical invention) gave a magical and ominous aspect to the wild abode.

The Hebrew cast himself on a couch of furs; and as the old man entered and closed the door, "Ximen," said he, "fill out wine, — it is a soothing counsellor, and I need it."

Extracting from one of the recesses of the cavern a flask and goblet, Ximen offered to his lord a copious draught of the sparkling vintage of the Vega, which seemed to invigorate and restore him.

"Old man," said he, concluding the potation with a deep-drawn sigh, "fill to thyself, — drink till thy veins feel young."

Ximen obeyed the mandate but imperfectly; the wine just
touched his lips, and the goblet was put aside.

"Ximen," resumed the Israelite, "how many of our race
have been butchered by the avarice of the Moorish kings
since first thou didst set foot within the city?"

"Three thousand.   The number was completed last winter,
by the order of Jusef the vizier; and their goods and coffers
are transformed into shafts and cimeters against the dogs of
Galilee."

"Three thousand, — no more? Three thousand only? I
would the number had been tripled, for the interest is becom-
ing due."

"My brother and my son and my grandson are among the
number," said the old man, and his face grew yet more
deathlike.

"Their monuments shall be in hecatombs of their tyrants.
They shall not, at least, call the Jews niggards in revenge."

"But pardon me, noble chief of a fallen people, thinkest
thou we shall be less despoiled and trodden under foot by yon
haughty and stiff-necked Nazarenes than by the Arabian
misbelievers?"

"Accursed, in truth, are both," returned the Hebrew; "but
the one promise more fairly than the other.   I have seen this
Ferdinand and his proud queen; they are pledged to accord
us rights and immunities we have never known before in
Europe."

"And they will not touch our traffic, our gains, our gold?"

"Out on thee!" cried the fiery Israelite, stamping on the
ground. "I would all the gold of earth were sunk into the
everlasting pit! It is this mean and miserable and loathsome
leprosy of avarice that gnaws away from our whole race the
heart, the soul, nay, the very form, of man! Many a time,
when I have seen the lordly features of the descendants of
Solomon and Joshua (features that stamp the nobility of the
Eastern world, born to mastery and command) sharpened and
furrowed by petty cares; when I have looked upon the frame
of the strong man bowed, like a crawling reptile, to some
huckstering bargainer of silks and unguents, and heard the

voice, that should be raising the battle-cry, smoothed into fawning accents of base fear or yet baser hope, — I have asked myself if I am indeed of the blood of Israel, and thanked the great Jehovah that he hath spared me at least the curse that hath blasted my brotherhood into usurers and slaves!"

Ximen prudently forbore an answer to enthusiasm which he neither shared nor understood; but, after a brief silence, turned back the stream of the conversation.

"You resolve, then, upon prosecuting vengeance on the Moors, at whatsoever hazard of the broken faith of these Nazarenes?"

"Ay, the vapour of human blood hath risen unto heaven, and, collected into thunder-clouds, hangs over the doomed and guilty city. And now, Ximen, I have a new cause for hatred to the Moors: the flower that I have reared and watched, the spoiler hath sought to pluck it from my hearth. Leila, thou hast guarded her ill, Ximen; and wert thou not endeared to me by thy very malice and vices, the rising sun should have seen thy trunk on the waters of the Darro."

"My lord," replied Ximen, "if thou, the wisest of our people, canst not guard a maiden from love, how canst thou see crime in the dull eyes and numbed senses of a miserable old man?"

The Israelite did not answer, nor seem to hear this deprecatory remonstrance. He appeared rather occupied with his own thoughts; and, speaking to himself, he muttered: "It must be so. The sacrifice is hard, the danger great, but here, at least, it is more immediate. It shall be done. Ximen," he continued, speaking aloud, "dost thou feel assured that even mine own countrymen, mine own tribe, know me not as one of them? Were my despised birth and religion published, my limbs would be torn asunder as an impostor, and all the arts of the Cabala could not save me."

"Doubt not, great master; none in Granada, save thy faithful Ximen, know thy secret."

"So let me dream and hope. And now to my work; for this night must be spent in toil."

The Hebrew drew before him some of the strange instruments we have described, and took from the recesses in the rock several scrolls. The old man lay at his feet, ready to obey his behests, but to all appearance rigid and motionless as the dead, whom his blanched hues and shrivelled form resembled. It was, indeed, as the picture of the enchanter at his work, and the corpse of some man of old, revived from the grave to minister to his spells and execute his commands.

Enough in the preceding conversation has transpired to convince the reader that the Hebrew, in whom he has already detected the Almamen of the Alhambra, was of no character common to his tribe. Of a lineage that shrouded itself in the darkness of his mysterious people in their day of power, and possessed of immense wealth which threw into poverty the resources of Gothic princes, the youth of that remarkable man had been spent, not in traffic and merchandise, but travel and study.

As a child, his home had been in Granada. He had seen his father butchered by the late king, Muley Abul Hassan, without other crime than his reputed riches, and his body literally cut open, to search for the jewels it was supposed he had swallowed. He saw and, boy as he was, he vowed revenge. A distant kinsman bore the orphan to lands more secure from persecution; and the art with which the Jews concealed their wealth, scattering it over various cities, had secured to Almamen the treasures the tyrant of Granada had failed to grasp.

He had visited the greater part of the world then known, and resided for many years at the court of the sultan of that hoary Egypt which still retained its fame for abstruse science and magic lore. He had not in vain applied himself to such tempting and wild researches, and had acquired many of those secrets now perhaps lost forever to the world. We do not mean to intimate that he attained to what legend and superstition impose upon our faith as the art of sorcery. He could neither command the elements nor pierce the veil of the future, — scatter armies with a word, nor pass from spot to spot by the utterance of a charmed formula. But men who for ages had passed their lives in attempting all the effects that can astonish and awe the vulgar, could not but learn some secrets which all the more sober wisdom of modern times would search ineffectually to solve or to revive. And many of such arts, acquired mechanically (their invention often the work of a chemical accident), those who attained to them could not always explain, nor account for the phenomena they created, so that the mightiness of their own deceptions deceived themselves; and they often believed they were the masters of the Nature to which they were, in reality, but erratic and wild disciples. Of such was the student in that grim cavern. He was in some measure the dupe, partly of his own bewildered wisdom, partly of the fervour of an imagination exceedingly high-wrought and enthusiastic. His own gorgeous vanity intoxicated him; and if it be an historical truth that the kings of the ancient world, blinded by their own power, had moments in which they believed themselves more than men, it is not incredible that sages, elevated even above kings, should conceive a frenzy as weak, or, it may be, as sublime, and imagine that they did not claim in vain the awful dignity with which the faith of the multitude invested their faculties and gifts.

But though the accident of birth, which excluded him from all field for energy and ambition, had thus directed the powerful mind of Almamen to contemplation and study, Nature had never intended passions so fierce for the calm, though visionary, pursuits to which he was addicted. Amidst scrolls and seers he had pined for action and glory; and baffled in all wholesome egress by the universal exclusion which, in every land and from every faith, met the religion he belonged to, the faculties within him ran riot, producing gigantic, but baseless schemes, which, as one after the other crumbled away, left behind feelings of dark misanthropy and intense revenge.

Perhaps, had his religion been prosperous and powerful, he might have been a sceptic: persecution and affliction made him a fanatic. Yet, true to that prominent characteristic of the old Hebrew race which made them look to a Messiah only as a warrior and a prince, and which taught them to associate all their hopes and schemes with worldly victories and power, Almamen desired rather to advance, than to obey, his religion. He cared little for its precepts, he thought little of its doctrines; but, night and day, he revolved his schemes for its earthly restoration and triumph.

At that time the Moors in Spain were far more deadly persecutors of the Jews than the Christians were. Amidst the Spanish cities on the coast that merchant tribe had formed commercial connections with the Christians sufficiently beneficial, both to individuals and to communities, to obtain for them, not only toleration, but something of personal friendship, wherever men bought and sold in the market-place. And the gloomy fanaticism which afterwards stained the fame of the great Ferdinand, and introduced the horrors of the Inquisition, had not yet made itself more than fitfully visible. But the Moors had treated this unhappy people with a wholesale and relentless barbarity. At Granada, under the reign of the fierce father of Boabdil, — "that king with the tiger heart," — the Jews had been literally placed without the pale of humanity; and even under the mild and contemplative Boabdil himself they had been plundered without mercy, and if suspected of secreting their treasures, massacred without scruple: the wants of the State continued their unrelenting accusers, — their wealth, their inexpiable crime.

It was in the midst of these barbarities that Almamen, for the first time since the day when the death-shriek of his agonized father rang in his ears, suddenly returned to Granada. He saw the unmitigated miseries of his brethren, and he remembered and repeated his vow. His name changed, his kindred dead, none remembered, in the mature Almamen, the beardless child of Issachar the Jew. He had long, indeed, deemed it advisable to disguise his faith, and was known throughout the African kingdoms but as the potent santon, or the wise magician.

This fame soon lifted him, in Granada, high in the councils of the court. Admitted to the intimacy of Muley Hassan, with Boabdil and the queen-mother he had conspired against that monarch, and had lived at least to avenge his father upon the royal murderer. He was no less intimate with Boabdil; but steeled against fellowship or affection for all men out of the pale of his faith, he saw in the confidence of the king only the blindness of a victim.

Serpent as he was, he cared not through what mire of treachery and fraud he trailed his baleful folds, so that at last he could spring upon his prey. Nature had given him sagacity and strength. The curse of circumstance had humbled, but reconciled him to the dust. He had the crawl of the reptile, — he had also its poison and its fangs.

CHAPTER VI.

THE LION IN THE NET.

IT was the next night, not long before daybreak, that the king of Granada abruptly summoned to his council Jusef, his vizier. The old man found Boabdil in great disorder and excitement; but he almost deemed his sovereign mad when he received from him the order to seize upon the person of Muza Ben Abil Gazan and to lodge him in the strongest dungeon of the Vermilion Tower. Presuming upon Boabdil's natural mildness, the vizier ventured to remonstrate, to suggest the danger of laying violent hands upon a chief so beloved, and to inquire what cause should be assigned for the outrage.

The veins swelled like cords upon Boabdil's brow as he listened to the vizier, and his answer was short and peremptory: —

"Am I yet a king, that I should fear a subject or excuse my will? Thou hast my orders; there are my signet and the firman: obedience, or the bow-string!"

Never before had Boabdil so resembled his dread father in speech and air; the vizier trembled to the soles of his feet,

and withdrew in silence. Boabdil watched him depart; and
then, clasping his hands in great emotion, exclaimed, "O lips
of the dead, ye have warned me, and to you I sacrifice the
friend of my youth!"

On quitting Boabdil, the vizier, taking with him some of
those foreign slaves of a seraglio who know no sympathy with
human passion outside its walls, bent his way to the palace
of Muza, sorely puzzled and perplexed. He did not, however,
like to venture upon the hazard of the alarm it might occasion
throughout the neighbourhood if he endeavoured, at so unsea-
sonable an hour, to force an entrance. He resolved, rather,
with his train, to wait at a little distance till, with the growing dawn, the gates should be unclosed and the inmates of the
palace astir.

Accordingly, cursing his stars and wondering at his mission, Jusef and his silent and ominous attendants concealed
themselves in a small copse adjoining the palace until the
daylight fairly broke over the awakened city. He then passed
into the palace, and was conducted to a hall where he found
the renowned Moslem already astir, and conferring with some
Zegri captains upon the tactics of a sortie designed for that
day.

It was with so evident a reluctance and apprehension that
Jusef approached the prince that the fierce and quick-sighted
Zegris instantly suspected some evil intention in his visit;
and when Muza, in surprise, yielded to the prayer of the
vizier for a private audience, it was with scowling brows and
sparkling eyes that the Moorish warriors left the darling of
the nobles alone with the messenger of their king.

"By the tomb of the prophet," said one of the Zegris as he
quitted the hall, "the timid Boabdil suspects our Ben Abil
Gazan. I learned of this before."

"Hush!" said another of the band; "let us watch. If the
king touch a hair of Muza's head, Allah have mercy on his
sins!"

Meanwhile, the vizier, in silence, showed to Muza the
firman and the signet; and then, without venturing to announce the place to which he was commissioned to conduct

the prince, besought him to follow at once. Muza changed colour, but not with fear.

"Alas!" said he, in a tone of deep sorrow, "can it be that I have fallen under my royal kinsman's suspicion or displeasure? But no matter; proud to set to Granada an example of valour in her defence, be it mine to set also an example of obedience to her king. Go on, I will follow thee. Yet stay,— you will have no need of guards; let us depart by a private egress: the Zegris might misgive, did they see me leave the palace with you at the very time the army are assembling in the Vivarrambla, and awaiting my presence. This way."

Thus saying, Muza, who, fierce as he was, obeyed every impulse that the Oriental loyalty dictated from a subject to a king, passed from the hall to a small door that admitted into the garden, and in thoughtful silence accompanied the vizier towards the Alhambra. As they passed the copse in which Muza, two nights before, had met with Almamen, the Moor, lifting his head suddenly, beheld fixed upon him the dark eyes of the magician as he emerged from the trees. Muza thought there was in those eyes a malign and hostile exultation; but Almamen, gravely saluting him, passed on through the grove. The prince did not deign to look back, or he might once more have encountered that withering gaze.

"Proud heathen," muttered Almamen to himself, "thy father filled his treasuries from the gold of many a tortured Hebrew; and even thou, too haughty to be the miser, hast been savage enough to play the bigot. Thy name is a curse in Israel; yet dost thou lust after the daughter of our despised race, and could defeated passion sting thee, I were avenged. Ay, sweep on, with thy stately step and lofty crest, — thou goest to chains, perhaps to death."

As Almamen thus vented his bitter spirit, the last gleam of the white robes of Muza vanished from his gaze. He paused a moment, turned away abruptly, and said, half aloud, "Vengeance, not on one man only, but on a whole race! Now for the Nazarene."

BOOK II.

CHAPTER I.

OUR narrative now summons us to the Christian army, and
to the tent in which the Spanish king held nocturnal counsel
with some of his more confidential warriors and advisers.
Ferdinand had taken the field with all the pomp and circumstance of a tournament rather than of a campaign, and his
pavilion literally blazed with purple and cloth of gold.

The king sat at the head of a table on which were scattered
maps and papers; nor in countenance and mien did that great
and politic monarch seem unworthy of the brilliant chivalry
by which he was surrounded. His black hair, richly perfumed
and anointed, fell in long locks on either side of a high,
imperial brow, upon whose calm though not unfurrowed surface the physiognomist would in vain have sought to read the
inscrutable heart of kings. His features were regular and
majestic, and his mantle, clasped with a single jewel of rare
price and lustre, and wrought at the breast with a silver cross,
waved over a vigorous and manly frame, which derived from
the composed and tranquil dignity of habitual command that
imposing effect which many of the renowned knights and
heroes in his presence took from loftier stature and ampler
proportions. At his right hand sat Prince Juan, his son, in
the first bloom of youth; at his left, the celebrated Rodrigo
Ponce de Leon, Marquis of Cadiz; along the table, in the
order of their military rank, were seen the splendid Duke of
Medina Sidonia, equally noble in aspect and in name, the
worn and thoughtful countenance of the Marquis de Villena

(the Bayard of Spain), the melancholy brow of the heroic
Alonzo de Aguilar, and the gigantic frame, the animated features, and sparkling eyes of that fiery Hernando del Pulgar
surnamed "the knight of the exploits."

"You see, señores," said the king, continuing an address to
which his chiefs seemed to listen with reverential attention,
"our best hope of speedily gaining the city is rather in the
dissensions of the Moors than our own sacred arms. The
walls are strong, the population still numerous, and under
Muza Ben Abil Gazan the tactics of the hostile army are, it
must be owned, administered with such skill as to threaten
very formidable delays to the period of our conquest. Avoiding the hazard of a fixed battle, the infidel cavalry harass our
camp by perpetual skirmishes; and in the mountain defiles
our detachments cannot cope with their light horse and treach-
erous ambuscades. It is true that by dint of time, by the
complete devastation of the Vega, and by vigilant prevention
of convoys from the sea-towns, we might starve the city into
yielding. But alas! my lords, our enemies are scattered and
numerous, and Granada is not the only place before which
the standard of Spain should be unfurled. Thus situated, the
lion does not disdain to serve himself of the fox; and, fortunately, we have now in Granada an ally that fights for us. I
have actual knowledge of all that passes within the Alhambra. The king yet remains in his palace, irresolute and
dreaming; and I trust that an intrigue by which his jealousies
are aroused against his general, Muza, may end either in the
loss of that able leader, or in the commotion of open rebellion
or civil war. Treason within Granada will open its gates
to us."

"Sire," said Ponce de Leon, after a pause, "under your
counsels I no more doubt of seeing our banner float above the
Vermilion Towers than I doubt the rising of the sun over
yonder hills; it matters little whether we win by stratagem
or force. But I need not say to your Highness that we should
carefully beware lest we be amused by inventions of the enemy,
and trust to conspiracies which may be but lying tales to blunt
our sabres and paralyze our action."

"Bravely spoken, wise De Leon!" exclaimed Hernando del Pulgar, hotly; "and against these infidels, aided by the cunning of the Evil One, methinks our best wisdom lies in the sword-arm. Well says our old Castilian proverb, —

> "'Curse them devoutly,
> Hammer them stoutly.'"

The king smiled slightly at the ardour of the favourite of his army, but looked round for more deliberate counsel.

"Sire," said Villena, "far be it from us to inquire the grounds upon which your Majesty builds your hope of dissension among the foe; but, placing the most sanguine confidence in a wisdom never to be deceived, it is clear that we should relax no energy within our means, but fight while we plot, and seek to conquer, while we do not neglect to undermine."

"You speak well, my lord," said Ferdinand, thoughtfully; "and you yourself shall head a strong detachment to-morrow to lay waste the Vega. Seek me two hours hence; the council for the present is dissolved."

The knights rose, and withdrew with the usual grave and stately ceremonies of respect which Ferdinand observed to, and exacted from, his court. The young prince remained.

"Son," said Ferdinand, when they were alone, "early and betimes should the Infants of Spain be lessoned in the science of kingcraft. These nobles are among the brightest jewels of the crown; but still, it is in the crown and for the crown that their light should sparkle. Thou seest how hot and fierce and warlike are the chiefs of Spain, — excellent virtues when manifested against our foes; but had we no foes, Juan, such virtues might cause us exceeding trouble. By Saint Jago, I have founded a mighty monarchy! Observe how it should be maintained, — by science, Juan, by science; and science is as far removed from brute force as this sword from a crowbar. Thou seemest bewildered and amazed, my son; thou hast heard that I seek to conquer Granada by dissensions among the Moors: when Granada is conquered, remember that the nobles themselves are at Granada. Ave Maria!

blessed be the Holy Mother, under whose eyes are the hearts of kings!"

Ferdinand crossed himself devoutly; and then, rising, drew aside a part of the drapery of the pavilion, and called in a low voice the name of Perez. A grave Spaniard, somewhat past the verge of middle age, appeared.

"Perez," said the king, reseating himself, "has the person we expected from Granada yet arrived?"

"Sire, yes, accompanied by a maiden."

"He hath kept his word; admit them. Ha! holy father, thy visits are always as balsam to the heart."

"Save you, my son!" returned a man in the robes of a Dominican friar, who had entered suddenly and without ceremony by another part of the tent, and who now seated himself with smileless composure at a little distance from the king.

There was a dead silence for some moments; and Perez still lingered within the tent, as if in doubt whether the entrance of the friar would not prevent or delay obedience to the king's command. On the calm face of Ferdinand himself appeared a slight shade of discomposure and irresolution, when the monk thus resumed, —

"My presence, my son, will not, I trust, disturb your conference with the infidel, since you deem that worldly policy demands your parley with the men of Belial."

"Doubtless not, doubtless not," returned the king, quickly; then, muttering to himself, "How wondrously doth this holy man penetrate into all our movements and designs!" he added aloud, "Let the messenger enter."

Perez bowed and withdrew.

During this time the young prince reclined in listless silence on his seat, and on his delicate features was an expression of weariness which augured but ill of his fitness for the stern business to which the lessons of his wise father were intended to educate his mind. His, indeed, was the age and his the soul for pleasure: the tumult of the camp was to him but a holiday exhibition; the march of an army, the exhilaration of a spectacle; the court as a banquet; the throne, the best seat at the entertainment. The life of the heir-apparent, to the life of the king possessive, is as the distinction between enchanting hope and tiresome satiety.

The small gray eyes of the friar wandered over each of his royal companions with a keen and penetrating glance, and then settled in the aspect of humility on the rich carpets that bespread the floor; nor did he again lift them till Perez, reappearing, admitted to the tent the Israelite, Almamen, accompanied by a female figure, whose long veil, extending from head to foot, could conceal neither the beautiful proportions nor the trembling agitation of her frame.

"When last, great king, I was admitted to thy presence," said Almamen, "thou didst make question of the sincerity and faith of thy servant; thou didst ask me for a surety of my faith; thou didst demand a hostage, and didst refuse further parley without such pledge were yielded to thee. Lo, I place under thy kingly care this maiden, — the sole child of my house, — as surety of my truth; I intrust to thee a life dearer than my own."

"You have kept faith with us, stranger," said the king, in that soft and musical voice which well disguised his deep craft and his unrelenting will, "and the maiden whom you intrust to our charge shall be ranked with the ladies of our royal consort."

"Sire," replied Almamen, with touching earnestness, "you now hold the power of life and death over all for whom this heart can breathe a prayer or cherish a hope, save for my countrymen and my religion. This solemn pledge between thee and me I render up without scruple, without fear. *To* thee I give a hostage, — *from* thee I have but a promise."

"But it is the promise of a king, a Christian, and a knight," said the king, with dignity rather mild than arrogant; "among monarchs, what hostage can be more sacred? Let this pass. How proceed affairs in the rebel city?"

"May this maiden withdraw ere I answer my lord the king?" said Almamen.

The young prince started to his feet. "Shall I conduct

this new charge to my mother?" he asked in a low voice, addressing Ferdinand.

The king half smiled. "The holy father were a better guide," he returned, in the same tone. But though the Dominican heard the hint, he retained his motionless posture; and Ferdinand, after a momentary gaze on the friar, turned away. "Be it so, Juan," said he, with a look meant to convey caution to the prince; "Perez shall accompany you to the queen. Return the moment your mission is fulfilled, — we want your presence."

While this conversation was carried on between the father and son, the Hebrew was whispering, in his sacred tongue, words of comfort and remonstrance to the maiden; but they appeared to have but little of the desired effect, and suddenly falling on his breast, she wound her arms around the Hebrew, whose breast shook with strong emotions, and exclaimed passionately, in the same language: "Oh, my father, what have I done? Why send me from thee? Why intrust thy child to the stranger? Spare me, spare me!"

"Child of my heart," returned the Hebrew, with solemn but tender accents, "even as Abraham offered up his son, must I offer thee upon the altars of our faith; but, O Leila! even as the angel of the Lord forbade the offering, so shall thy youth be spared, and thy years reserved for the glory of generations yet unborn. King of Spain," he continued, in the Spanish tongue, suddenly and eagerly, "you are a father; forgive my weakness, and speed this parting."

Juan approached, and with respectful courtesy attempted to take the hand of the maiden.

"You?" said the Israelite, with a dark frown. "O king! the prince is young."

"Honour knoweth no distinction of age," answered the king. "What ho, Perez! accompany this maiden and the prince to the queen's pavilion."

The sight of the sober years and grave countenance of the attendant seemed to reassure the Hebrew. He strained Leila in his arms, printed a kiss upon her forehead without removing her veil, and then, placing her almost in the arms of

Perez, turned away to the farther end of the tent, and concealed his face with his hands. The king appeared touched, but the Dominican gazed upon the whole scene with a sour scowl.

Leila still paused for a moment; and then, as if recovering her self-possession, said aloud and distinctly, "Man deserts me, but I will not forget that God is over all." Shaking off the hand of the Spaniard, she continued: "Lead on; I follow thee!" and left the tent with a steady and even majestic step.

"And now," said the king, when alone with the Dominican and Almamen, "how proceed our hopes?"

"Boabdil," replied the Israelite, "is aroused against both his army and their leader, Muza: the king will not quit the Alhambra; and this morning, ere I left the city, Muza himself was in the prisons of the palace."

"How?" cried the king, starting from his seat.

"This is my work," pursued the Hebrew, coldly. "It is these hands that are shaping for Ferdinand of Spain the keys of Granada."

"And right kingly shall be your guerdon," said the Spanish monarch. "Meanwhile, accept this earnest of our favour."

So saying, he took from his breast a chain of massive gold, the links of which were curiously inwrought with gems, and extended it to the Israelite. Almamen moved not. A dark flush upon his countenance bespoke the feelings he with difficulty restrained.

"I sell not my foes for gold, great king," said he, with a stern smile; "I sell my foes to buy the ransom of my friends."

"Churlish," said Ferdinand, offended; "but speak on, man, speak on!"

"If I place Granada, ere two weeks are past, within thy power, what shall be my reward?"

"Thou didst talk to me, when last we met, of immunities to the Jews."

The calm Dominican looked up as the king spoke, crossed himself, and resumed his attitude of humility.

"I demand for the people of Israel," returned Almamen, "free leave to trade and abide within the city and follow their callings, subjected only to the same laws and the same imposts as the Christian population."

"The same laws and the same imposts! Humph! there are difficulties in the concession. If we refuse?"

"Our treaty is ended. Give me back the maiden, — you will have no further need of the hostage you demanded. I return to the city, and renew our interviews no more."

Politic and cold-blooded as was the temperament of the great Ferdinand, he had yet the imperious and haughty nature of a prosperous and long-descended king; and he bit his lip in deep displeasure at the tone of the dictatorial and stately stranger.

"Thou usest plain language, my friend," said he. "My words can be as rudely spoken: thou art in my power, and canst return not, save at my permission."

"I have your royal word, sire, for free entrance and safe egress," answered Almamen. "Break it, and Granada is with the Moors till the Darro runs red with the blood of her heroes, and her people strew the vales as the leaves in autumn."

"Art thou then thyself of the Jewish faith?" asked the king. "If thou art not, wherefore are the outcasts of the world so dear to thee?"

"My fathers were of that creed, royal Ferdinand; and if I myself desert their creed, I do not desert their cause. O king! are my terms scorned or accepted?"

"I accept them, provided, first, that thou obtainest the exile or death of Muza; secondly, that within two weeks of this date thou bringest me, along with the chief councillors of Granada, the written treaty of the capitulation and the keys of the city. Do this, and though the sole king in Christendom who dares the hazard, I offer to the Israelites throughout Andalusia the common laws and rights of citizens of Spain, and to thee I will accord such dignity as may content thy ambition."

The Hebrew bowed reverently, and drew from his breast a scroll, which he placed on the table before the king.

"This writing, mighty Ferdinand, contains the articles of our compact."

"How, knave! wouldst thou have us commit our royal signature to conditions with such as thou art, to the chance of the public eye? The king's word is the king's bond."

The Hebrew took up the scroll with imperturbable composure. "My child!" said he. "Will your Majesty summon back my child? We would depart."

"A sturdy mendicant this, by the Virgin!" muttered the king; and then, speaking aloud, "Give me the paper, I will scan it."

Running his eyes hastily over the words, Ferdinand paused a moment, and then drew towards him the implements of writing, signed the scroll, and returned it to Almamen.

The Israelite kissed it thrice with Oriental veneration, and replaced it in his breast.

Ferdinand looked at him hard and curiously. He was a profound reader of men's characters; but that of his guest baffled and perplexed him.

"And how, stranger," said he, gravely, — "how can I trust that man who thus distrusts one king and sells another?"

"O king!" replied Almamen (accustomed from his youth to commune with and command the possessors of thrones yet more absolute), — "O king! if thou believest me actuated by personal and selfish interests in this our compact, thou hast but to make my service minister to my interest, and the lore of human nature will tell thee that thou has won a ready and submissive slave. But if thou thinkest I have avowed sentiments less abject, and developed qualities higher than those of the mere bargainer for sordid power, oughtest thou not to rejoice that chance has thrown into thy way one whose intellect and faculties may be made thy tool? If I betray another, that other is my deadly foe. Dost not thou, the lord of armies, betray thine enemy? The Moor is an enemy bitterer to myself than to thee. Because I betray an enemy, am I unworthy to serve a friend? If I, a single man and a stranger to the Moor, can yet command the secrets of palaces and render vain the counsels of armed men, have I not in that attested that I am one of whom a wise king can make an able servant?"

"Thou art a subtle reasoner, my friend," said Ferdinand, smiling gently. "Peace go with thee! our conference for the time is ended. What ho, Perez!"

The attendant appeared.

"Thou hast left the maiden with the queen?"

"Sire, you have been obeyed."

"Conduct this stranger to the guard who led him through the camp. He quits us under the same protection. Farewell! Yet stay, — thou art assured that Muza Ben Abil Gazan is in the prisons of the Moor?"

"Yes."

"Blessed be the Virgin!"

"Thou hast heard our conference, Father Tomas?" said the king, anxiously, when the Hebrew had withdrawn.

"I have, son."

"Did thy veins freeze with horror?"

"Only when my son signed the scroll. It seemed to me then that I saw the cloven foot of the tempter."

"Tush, father! the tempter would have been more wise than to reckon upon a faith which no ink and no parchment can render valid, if the Church absolve the compact. Thou understandest me, father?"

"I do. I know your pious heart and well-judging mind."

"Thou wert right," resumed the king, musingly, "when thou didst tell us that these caitiff Jews were waxing strong in the fatness of their substance. They would have equal laws, the insolent blasphemers!"

"Son!" said the Dominican, with earnest adjuration, "God, who has prospered your arms and councils, will require at your hands an account of the power intrusted to you. Shall there be no difference between His friends and His foes, — His disciples and His crucifiers?"

"Priest," said the king, laying his hand on the monk's shoulder, and with a saturnine smile upon his countenance, "were religion silent in this matter, policy has a voice loud enough to make itself heard. The Jews demand equal rights: when men demand equality with their masters, treason is at work, and Justice sharpens her sword. Equality! these wealthy usurers! Sacred Virgin, they would be soon buying up our kingdoms."

The Dominican gazed hard on the king. "Son, I trust thee," he said, in a low voice, and glided from the tent.

CHAPTER II.

THE AMBUSH, THE STRIFE, AND THE CAPTURE.

THE dawn was slowly breaking over the wide valley of Granada as Almamen pursued his circuitous and solitary path back to the city. He was now in a dark and entangled hollow, covered with brakes and bushes, from amidst which tall forest trees rose in frequent intervals, gloomy and breathless in the still morning air. As, emerging from this jungle, if so it may be called, the towers of Granada gleamed upon him, a human countenance peered from the shade, and Almamen started to see two dark eyes fixed upon his own.

He halted abruptly and put his hand on his dagger, when a low, sharp whistle from the apparition before him was answered around, behind; and ere he could draw breath, the Israelite was begirt by a group of Moors in the garb of peasants.

"Well, my masters," said Almamen, calmly, as he encountered the wild, savage countenances that glared upon him, "think you there is aught to fear from the solitary santon?"

"It is the magician," whispered one man to his neighbour, — "let him pass."

"Nay," was the answer, "take him before the captain; we have orders to seize upon all we meet."

This counsel prevailed; and gnashing his teeth with secret rage, Almamen found himself hurried along by the peasants through the thickest part of the copse. At length the procession stopped in a semicircular patch of rank sward, in which several head of cattle were quietly grazing, and a yet more numerous troop of peasants reclined around upon the grass.

"Whom have we here?" asked a voice which startled back the dark blood from Almamen's cheek; and a Moor of commanding presence rose from the midst of his brethren. "By the beard of the Prophet, it is the false santon! What dost thou from Granada at this hour?"

"Noble Muza," returned Almamen, — who, though indeed amazed that one whom he had imagined his victim was thus unaccountably become his judge, retained, at least, the semblance of composure, — "my answer is to be given only to my lord the king; it is his commands that I obey."

"Thou art aware," said Muza, frowning, "that thy life is forfeited without appeal? Whatsoever inmate of Granada is found without the walls between sunrise and sunset, dies the death of a traitor and deserter."

"The servants of the Alhambra are excepted," answered the Israelite, without changing countenance.

"Ah," muttered Muza, as a painful and sudden thought seemed to cross him, "can it be possible that the rumour of the city has truth, and that the monarch of Granada is in treaty with the foe?" He mused a little; and then, motioning the Moors to withdraw, he continued aloud: "Almamen, answer me truly: hast thou sought the Christian camp with any message from the king?"

"I have not."

"Art thou without the walls on the mission of the king?"

"If I be so, I am a traitor to the king should I reveal his secret."

"I doubt thee much, santon," said Muza, after a pause; "I know thee for my enemy, and I do believe thy counsels have poisoned the king's ear against me, his people, and his duties. But no matter; thy life is spared a while. Thou remainest with us, and with us shalt thou return to the king."

"But, noble Muza —"

"I have said! Guard the santon; mount him upon one of our chargers: he shall abide with us in our ambush."

While Almamen chafed in vain at his arrest, all in the

Christian camp was yet still. At length, as the sun began to lift himself above the mountains, first a murmur, and then a din, betokened warlike preparations. Several parties of horse, under gallant and experienced leaders, formed themselves in different quarters, and departed in different ways, on expeditions of forage, or in the hope of skirmish with the straggling detachments of the enemy. Of these, the best equipped was conducted by the Marquis de Villena and his gallant brother, Don Alonzo de Pacheco. In this troop, too, rode many of the best blood of Spain; for in that chivalric army the officers vied with each other who should most eclipse the meaner soldiery in feats of personal valour, and the name of Villena drew around him the eager and ardent spirits that pined at the general inactivity of Ferdinand's politic campaign.

The sun, now high in heaven, glittered on the splendid arms and gorgeous pennons of Villena's company as, leaving the camp behind, it entered a rich and wooded district that skirts the mountain barrier of the Vega. The brilliancy of the day, the beauty of the scene, the hope and excitement of enterprise, animated the spirits of the whole party. In these expeditions strict discipline was often abandoned, from the certainty that it could be resumed at need. Conversation, gay and loud, interspersed at times with snatches of song, was heard amongst the soldiery; and in the nobler group that rode with Villena, there was even less of the proverbial gravity of Spaniards.

"Now, Marquis," said Don Estevon de Suzon, "what wager shall be between us as to which lance this day robs Moorish beauty of the greatest number of its worshippers?"

"My falchion against your jennet," said Don Alonzo de Pacheco, taking up the challenge.

"Agreed. But, talking of beauty, were you in the queen's pavilion last night, noble marquis? It was enriched by a new maiden, whose strange and sudden apparition none can account for. Her eyes would have eclipsed the fatal glance of Cava; and had I been Rodrigo, I might have lost a crown for her smile."

"Ay," said Villena, "I heard of her beauty, — some hostage from one of the traitor Moors with whom the king (the saints bless him!) bargains for the city. They tell me the prince incurred the queen's grave rebuke for his attentions to the maiden."

"And this morning I saw that fearful Father Tomas steal into the prince's tent. I wish Don Juan well through the lecture. The monk's advice is like the *algarroba:* [1] when it is laid up to dry, it may be reasonably wholesome; but it is harsh and bitter enough when taken fresh."

At this moment one of the subaltern officers rode up to the marquis and whispered in his ear.

"Ha," said Villena, "the Virgin be praised! Sir Knights, booty is at hand. Silence! close the ranks."

With that, mounting a little eminence and shading his eyes with his hand, the marquis surveyed the plain below; and at some distance he beheld a horde of Moorish peasants driving some cattle into a thick copse. The word was hastily given, the troop dashed on, every voice was hushed, and the clatter of mail and the sound of hoofs alone broke the delicious silence of the noonday landscape. Ere they reached the copse, the peasants had disappeared within it. The marquis marshalled his men in a semicircle round the trees, and sent on a detachment to the rear, to cut off every egress from the wood. This done, the troop dashed within. For the first few yards the space was more open than they had anticipated; but the ground soon grew uneven, rugged, and almost precipitous, and the soil and the interlaced trees alike forbade any rapid motion to the horse. Don Alonzo de Pacheco, mounted on a charger whose agile and docile limbs had been tutored to every description of warfare, and himself of light weight and incomparable horsemanship, dashed on before the rest. The trees hid him for a moment; when suddenly a wild yell was heard, and as it ceased, up rose the solitary voice of the Spaniard, shouting, "Santiago, y cierra, España (Saint Jago, and charge, Spain)!"

Each cavalier spurred forward; when suddenly a shower of

[1] The algarroba is a sort of leguminous plant common in Spain.

darts and arrows rattled on their armour, and up sprung from bush and reeds and rocky clift a number of Moors, and with wild shouts swarmed around the Spaniards.

"Back for your lives," cried Villena; "we are beset! Make for the level ground!"

He turned, spurred from the thicket, and saw the Paynim foe emerging through the glen, line after line of man and horse, each Moor leading his slight and fiery steed by the bridle, and leaping on it as he issued from the wood into the plain. Cased in complete mail, his visor down, his lance in its rest, Villena (accompanied by such of his knights as could disentangle themselves from the Moorish foot) charged upon the foe. A moment of fierce shock passed: on the ground lay many a Moor, pierced through by the Christian lance, and on the other side of the foe was heard the voice of Villena: "Saint Jago to the rescue!" But the brave marquis stood almost alone, save his faithful chamberlain, Solier. Several of his knights were dismounted, and swarms of Moors, with lifted knives, gathered round them as they lay, searching for the joints of the armour, which might admit a mortal wound. Gradually, one by one, many of Villena's comrades joined their leader, and now the green mantle of Don Alonzo de Pacheco was seen waving without the copse, and Villena congratulated himself on the safety of his brother. Just at that moment a Moorish cavalier spurred from his troop and met Pacheco in full career. The Moor was not clad, as was the common custom of the Paynim nobles, in the heavy Christian armour; he wore the light, flexile mail of the ancient heroes of Araby or Fez. His turban, which was protected by chains of the finest steel interwoven with the folds, was of the most dazzling white; white also were his tunic and short mantle; on his left arm hung a short circular shield, in his right hand was poised a long and slender lance. As this Moor, mounted on a charger in whose raven hue not a white hair could be detected, dashed forward against Pacheco, both Christian and Moor breathed hard and remained passive. Either nation felt it as a sacrilege to thwart the encounter of champions so renowned.

"God save my brave brother!" muttered Villena, anxiously. "Amen!" said those around him; for all who had ever wit-nessed the wildest valour in that war trembled as they recog-nized the dazzling robe and coal-black charger of Muza Ben Abil Gazan. Nor was that renowned infidel mated with an unworthy foe. "Pride of the tournament, and terror of the war," was the favourite title which the knights and ladies of Castile had bestowed on Don Alonzo de Pacheco.

When the Spaniard saw the redoubted Moor approach, he halted abruptly for a moment; and then, wheeling his horse around, took a wider circuit, to give additional impetus to his charge. The Moor, aware of his purpose, halted also, and awaited the moment of his rush; when once more he darted forward, and the combatants met with a skill which called forth a cry of involuntary applause from the Christians them-selves. Muza received on the small surface of his shield the ponderous spear of Alonzo, while his own light lance struck upon the helmet of the Christian, and by the exactness of the aim, rather than the weight of the blow, made Alonzo reel in his saddle.

The lances were thrown aside; the long, broad falchion of the Christian, the curved Damascus cimeter of the Moor, gleamed in the air. They reined their chargers opposite each other in grave and deliberate silence.

"Yield thee, Sir Knight!" at length cried the fierce Moor; "for the motto on my cimeter declares that if thou meetest its stroke, thy days are numbered. The sword of the believer is the Key of Heaven and Hell." [1]

"False Paynim," answered Alonzo, in a voice that rang hollow through his helmet, "a Christian knight is the equal of a Moorish army!"

Muza made no reply, but left the rein of his charger on his neck; the noble animal understood the signal, and with a short, impatient cry rushed forward at full speed. Alonzo met the charge with his falchion upraised, and his whole body covered with his shield; the Moor bent, the Spaniards raised a shout, Muza seemed stricken from his horse. But the blow

---

[1] Such, says Sale, is the poetical phrase of the Mohammedan divines.

of the heavy falchion had not touched him; and, seemingly without an effort, the curved blade of his own cimeter, gliding by that part of his antagonist's throat where the helmet joins the cuirass, passed unresistingly and silently through the joints, and Alonzo fell at once, and without a groan, from his horse, — his armour, to all appearance, unpenetrated, while the blood oozed slow and gurgling from a mortal wound.

"Allah il Allah!" shouted Muza, as he joined his friends; "Lelilies! Lelilies!" echoed the Moors; and ere the Christians recovered their dismay, they were engaged hand to hand with their ferocious and swarming foes. It was, indeed, fearful odds, and it was a marvel to the Spaniards how the Moors had been enabled to harbour and conceal their numbers in so small a space. Horse and foot alike beset the company of Villena, already sadly reduced; and while the infantry, with desperate and savage fierceness, thrust themselves under the very bellies of the chargers, encountering both the hoofs of the steed and the deadly lance of the rider, in the hope of finding a vulnerable place for the sharp Moorish knife, the horsemen, avoiding the stern grapple of the Spanish warriors, harassed them by the shaft and lance, — now advancing, now retreating, and performing, with incredible rapidity, the evolutions of Oriental cavalry. But the life and soul of his party was the indomitable Muza. With a rashness which seemed to the superstitious Spaniards like the safety of a man protected by magic, he spurred his ominous black barb into the very midst of the serried phalanx which Villena endeavoured to form around him, breaking the order by his single charge, and from time to time bringing to the dust some champion of the troop by the noiseless and scarce-seen edge of his fatal cimeter.

Villena, in despair alike of fame and life, and gnawed with grief for his brother's loss, at length resolved to put the last hope of the battle on his single arm. He gave the signal for retreat; and to protect his troop, remained himself, alone and motionless, on his horse, like a statue of iron. Though not of large frame, he was esteemed the best swordsman, next only

to Hernando del Pulgar and Gonsalvo de Cordova, in the
army, — practised alike in the heavy assault of the Christian
warfare, and the rapid and dexterous exercise of the Moorish
cavalry. There he remained, alone and grim, — a lion at bay,
— while his troops slowly retreated down the Vega, and their
trumpets sounded loud signals of distress and demands for
succour to such of their companions as might be within hear-
ing. Villena's armour defied the shafts of the Moors; and as
one after one darted towards him, with whirling cimeter and
momentary assault, few escaped with impunity from an eye
equally quick and a weapon more than equally formidable.
Suddenly, a cloud of dust swept towards him; and Muza, a
moment before at the farther end of the field, came glittering
through that cloud, with his white robe waving and his right
arm bare. Villena recognized him, set his teeth hard, and
putting spurs to his charger, met the rush. Muza swerved
aside just as the heavy falchion swung over his head, and by
a back stroke of his own cimeter shore through the cuirass
just above the hip-joint, and the blood followed the blade.
The brave cavaliers saw the danger of their chief; three of
their number darted forward, and came in time to separate
the combatants.

Muza stayed not to encounter the new reinforcement; but
speeding across the plain, was soon seen rallying his own
scattered cavalry, and pouring them down, in one general
body, upon the scanty remnant of the Spaniards.

"Our day is come!" said the good knight Villena, with
bitter resignation. "Nothing is left for us, my friends, but
to give up our lives, — an example how Spanish warriors
should live and die. May God and the Holy Mother forgive
our sins and shorten our purgatory!"

Just as he spoke, a clarion was heard at a distance, and the
sharpened senses of the knights caught the ring of advancing
hoofs.

"We are saved!" cried Estevon de Suzon, rising on his
stirrups.

While he spoke, the dashing stream of the Moorish horse
broke over the little band, and Estevon beheld bent upon

himself the dark eyes and quivering lip of Muza Ben Abil Gazan. That noble knight had never, perhaps, till then known fear; but he felt his heart stand still as he now stood opposed to that irresistible foe.

"The dark fiend guides his blade!" thought De Suzon; "but I was shriven but yestermorn." The thought restored his wonted courage, and he spurred on to meet the cimeter of the Moor.

His assault took Muza by surprise. The Moor's horse stumbled over the ground, cumbered with the dead and slippery with blood, and his uplifted cimeter could not do more than break the force of the gigantic arm of De Suzon as the knight's falchion, bearing down the cimeter, and alighting on the turban of the Mohammedan, clove midway through its folds, arrested only by the admirable temper of the links of steel which protected it. The shock hurled the Moor to the ground; he rolled under the saddle-girths of his antagonist.

"Victory and Saint Jago!" cried the knight; "Muza is —"

The sentence was left eternally unfinished. The blade of the fallen Moor had already pierced De Suzon's horse through a mortal but undefended part. It fell, bearing his rider with him. A moment, and the two champions lay together grappling in the dust; in the next, the short knife which the Moor wore in his girdle had penetrated the Christian's vizor, passing through the brain.

To remount his steed, that remained at hand humbled and motionless, to appear again amongst the thickest of the fray, was a work no less rapidly accomplished than had been the slaughter of the unhappy Estevon de Suzon. But now the fortune of the day was stopped in a progress hitherto so triumphant to the Moors.

Pricking fast over the plain were seen the glittering horsemen of the Christian reinforcements; and at the remoter distance, the royal banner of Spain, indistinctly descried through volumes of dust, denoted that Ferdinand himself was advancing to the support of his cavaliers.

The Moors, however, who had themselves received **many**

and mysterious reinforcements, which seemed to spring up like magic from the bosom of the earth, — so suddenly and unexpectedly had they emerged from copse and cleft in that mountainous and entangled neighbourhood, — were not unprepared for a fresh foe. At the command of the vigilant Muza they drew off, fell into order, and seizing, while yet there was time, the vantage-ground which inequalities of the soil and the shelter of the trees gave to their darts and agile horse, they presented an array which Ponce de Leon himself, who now arrived, deemed it more prudent not to assault. While Villena, in accents almost inarticulate with rage, was urging the Marquis of Cadiz to advance, Ferdinand, surrounded by the flower of his court, arrived at the rear of the troops, and after a few words interchanged with Ponce de Leon, gave the signal of retreat.

When the Moors beheld that noble soldiery slowly breaking ground and retiring towards the camp, even Muza could not control their ardour. They rushed forward, harassing the retreat of the Christians, and delaying the battle by various skirmishes.

It was at this time that the headlong valour of Hernando del Pulgar, who had arrived with Ponce de Leon, distinguished itself in feats which yet live in the songs of Spain. Mounted upon an immense steed, and himself of colossal strength, he was seen charging alone upon the assailants, and scattering numbers to the ground with the sweep of his enormous two-handed falchion. With a loud voice he called on Muza to oppose him; but the Moor, fatigued with slaughter, and scarcely recovered from the shock of his encounter with De Suzon, reserved so formidable a foe for a future contest.

It was at this juncture, while the field was covered with straggling skirmishers, that a small party of Spaniards, in cutting their way to the main body of their countrymen through one of the numerous copses held by the enemy, fell in at the outskirt with an equal number of Moors, and engaged them in a desperate conflict, hand to hand. Amidst the infidels was one man who took no part in the affray. At a little distance, he gazed for a few moments upon the fierce and relentless slaughter of Moor and Christian with a smile of stern and complacent delight; and then, taking advantage of the general confusion, rode gently and, as he hoped, unobserved away from the scene. But he was not destined so quietly to escape. A Spaniard perceived him, and from something strange and unusual in his garb, judged him one of the Moorish leaders; and presently Almamen, for it was he, beheld before him the uplifted falchion of a foe neither disposed to give quarter nor to hear parley. Brave though the Israelite was, many reasons concurred to prevent his taking a personal part against the soldier of Spain; and seeing he should have no chance of explanation, he fairly put spurs to his horse and galloped across the plain. The Spaniard followed, gained upon him, and Almamen at length turned in despair and the wrath of his haughty nature.

"Have thy will, fool!" said he, between his grinded teeth, as he griped his dagger and prepared for the conflict. It was long and obstinate, for the Spaniard was skilful; and the Hebrew, wearing no mail, and without any weapon more formidable than a sharp and well-tempered dagger, was forced to act cautiously on the defensive. At length the combatants grappled, and by a dexterous thrust the short blade of Almamen pierced the throat of his antagonist, who fell prostrate to the ground.

"I am safe," he thought, as he wheeled round his horse; when lo, the Spaniards he had just left behind, and who had now routed their antagonists, were upon him.

"Yield, or die!" cried the leader of the troop.

Almamen glared round; no succour was at hand. "I am not your enemy," said he sullenly, throwing down his weapon, —"bear me to your camp."

A trooper seized his rein, and, scouring along, the Spaniards soon reached the retreating army.

Meanwhile the evening darkened, the shout and the roar grew gradually less and less loud. The battle had ceased; the stragglers had joined their several standards; and by the light of the first star the Moorish force, bearing their wounded

General View of the Alhambra from the Tower of Homenaje.

brethren, and elated with success, re-entered the gates of Granada as the black charger of the hero of the day, closing the rear of the cavalry, disappeared within the gloomy portals.

CHAPTER III.

THE HERO IN THE POWER OF THE DREAMER.

IT was in the same chamber, and nearly at the same hour, in which we first presented to the reader Boabdil el Chico that we are again admitted to the presence of that ill-starred monarch. He was not alone. His favourite slave, Amine, reclined upon the ottomans, gazing with anxious love upon his thoughtful countenance as he leaned against the glittering wall by the side of the casement, gazing abstractedly on the scene below.

From afar he heard the shouts of the populace at the return of Muza, and bursts of artillery confirmed the tidings of triumph which had already been borne to his ear.

"May the king live forever!" said Amine, timidly; "his armies have gone forth to conquer."

"But without their king," replied Boabdil, bitterly, "and headed by a traitor and a foe. I am meshed in the nets of an inextricable fate!"

"Oh," said the slave, with sudden energy, as, clasping her hands, she rose from her couch, — "oh, my lord, would that these humble lips dared utter other words than those of love!"

"And what wise counsel would they give me?" asked Boabdil, with a faint smile. "Speak on."

"I will obey thee, then, even if it displease," cried Amine; and she rose, her cheek glowing, her eyes sparkling, her beautiful form dilated. "I am a daughter of Granada, I am the beloved of a king; I will be true to my birth and to my fortunes.

Boabdil el Chico, the last of a line of heroes, shake off these gloomy fantasies, these doubts and dreams that smother the fire of a great nature and a kingly soul! Awake, arise, rob Granada of her Muza; be thyself her Muza! Trustest thou to magic and to spells? Then grave them on thy breastplate, write them on thy sword, and live no longer the Dreamer of the Alhambra, become the saviour of thy people!"

Boabdil turned and gazed on the inspired and beautiful form before him with mingled emotions of surprise and shame. "Out of the mouth of woman cometh my rebuke," said he, sadly. "It is well!"

"Pardon me, pardon me!" said the slave, falling humbly at his knees; "but blame me not that I would have thee worthy of thyself. Wert thou not happier, was not thy heart more light and thy hope more strong when, at the head of thine armies, thine own cimeter slew thine own foes, and the terror of the Hero-king spread, in flame and slaughter, from the mountains to the seas. Boabdil, dear as thou art to me, — equally as I would have loved thee hadst thou been born a lowly fisherman of the Darro, — since thou art a king, I would have thee die a king, even if my own heart broke as I armed thee for thy latest battle!"

"Thou knowest not what thou sayest, Amine," said Boabdil, "nor canst thou tell what spirits that are not of earth dictate to the actions and watch over the destinies of the rulers of nations. If I delay, if I linger, it is not from terror, but from wisdom. The cloud must gather on, dark and slow, ere the moment for the thunderbolt arrives."

"On thine own house will the thunderbolt fall, since over thine own house thou sufferest the cloud to gather," said a calm and stern voice.

Boabdil started; and in the chamber stood a third person, in the shape of a woman, past middle age, and of commanding port and stature. Upon her long-descending robes of embroidered purple were thickly woven jewels of royal price, and her dark hair, slightly tinged with gray, parted over a majestic brow, while a small diadem surmounted the folds of the turban.

"My mother," said Boabdil, with some haughty reserve in his tone, "your presence is unexpected."

"Ay," answered Ayxa la Horra, — for it was indeed that celebrated and haughty and high-souled queen, — "and unwelcome; so is ever that of your true friends. But not thus unwelcome was the presence of your mother when her brain and her hand delivered you from the dungeon in which your stern father had cast your youth, and the dagger and the bowl seemed the only keys that would unlock the cell."

"And better hadst thou left the ill-omened son that thy womb conceived to die thus in youth, honoured and lamented, than to live to manhood, wrestling against an evil star and a relentless fate."

"Son," said the queen, gazing upon him with lofty and half disdainful compassion, "men's conduct shapes out their own fortunes, and the unlucky are never the valiant and the wise."

"Madam," said Boabdil, colouring with passion, "I am still a king, nor will 1 be thus bearded. Withdraw!"

Ere the queen could reply, a eunuch entered, and whispered Boabdil.

"Ha!" said he, joyfully, stamping his foot, "comes he then to brave the lion in his den? Let the rebel look to it. Is he alone?"

"Alone, great king."

"Bid my guards wait without; let the slightest signal summon them. Amine, retire! Madam — "

"Son!" interrupted Ayxa la Horra, in visible agitation, "do I guess aright? Is the brave Muza, the sole bulwark and hope of Granada, whom unjustly thou wouldst last night have placed in chains (chains! Great Prophet, is it thus a king should reward his heroes?), — is, I say, Muza here, and wilt thou make him the victim of his own generous trust?"

"Retire, woman," said Boabdil, sullenly.

"I will not, save by force. I resisted a fiercer soul than thine when I saved thee from thy father."

"Remain, then, if thou wilt, and learn how kings can punish traitors. Mesnour, admit the hero of Granada."

Amine had vanished. Boabdil seated himself on the

cushions, his face calm but pale. The queen stood erect at a little distance, her arms folded on her breast, and her aspect knit and resolute. In a few moments Muza entered, alone. He approached the king with the profound salutation of Oriental obeisance, and then stood before him with down-cast eyes, in an attitude from which respect could not divorce a natural dignity and pride of mien.

"Prince," said Boabdil, after a moment's pause, "yester-morn, when I sent for thee, thou didst brave my orders. Even in mine own Alhambra thy minions broke out in mutiny; they surrounded the fortress in which thou wert to wait my pleas-ure; they intercepted, they insulted, they drove back my guards; they stormed the towers protected by the banner of thy king. The governor, a coward or a traitor, rendered thee to the rebellious crowd. Was this all? No, by the Prophet. Thou, by right my captive, didst leave thy prison but to head mine armies. And this day the traitor subject, the secret foe, was the leader of a people who defy a king. This night thou comest to me unsought. Thou feelest secure from my just wrath, even in my palace. Thine insolence blinds and betrays thee. Man, thou art in my power! Ho, there!"

As the king spoke, he rose; and presently the arcades at the back of the pavilion were darkened by long lines of the Ethiopian guard, each of height which, beside the slight Moorish race, appeared gigantic, — stolid and passionless machines, to execute, without thought, the bloodiest or the slightest caprice of despotism. There they stood, their silver breastplates and long earrings contrasting their dusky skins, and bearing over their shoulders immense clubs studded with brazen nails.

A little advanced from the rest stood the captain, with the fatal bowstring hanging carelessly on his arm, and his eyes intent to catch the slightest gesture of the king.

"Behold!" said Boabdil to his prisoner.

"I do, and am prepared for what I have foreseen."

The queen grew pale, but continued silent.

Muza resumed.

"Lord of the faithful!" said he, "if yestermorn I had acted otherwise, it would have been to the ruin of thy throne and our common race. The fierce Zegris suspected and learned my capture. They summoned the troops; they delivered me, it is true. At that time had I reasoned with them, it would have been as drops upon a flame. They were bent on besieging thy palace, — perhaps upon demanding thy abdication. I could not stifle their fury, but I could direct it. In the moment of passion I led them from rebellion against our common king to victory against our common foe. That duty done, I come, unscathed from the sword of the Christian, to bare my neck to the bowstring of my friend. Alone, untracked, unsuspected, I have entered thy palace, to prove to the sovereign of Granada that the defendant of his throne is not a rebel to his will. Now summon the guards; I have done."

"Muza," said Boabdil, in a softened voice, while he shaded his face with his hand, "we played together as children, and I have loved thee well. My kingdom even now, perchance, is passing from me; but I could almost be reconciled to that loss, if I thought thy loyalty had not left me."

"Dost thou in truth suspect the faith of Muza Ben Abil Gazan?" said the Moorish prince, in a tone of surprise and sorrow. "Unhappy king! I deemed that my services, and not my defection, made my crime."

"Why do my people hate me? Why do my armies menace?" said Boabdil, evasively. "Why should a subject possess that allegiance which a king cannot obtain?"

"Because," replied Muza, boldly, "the king has delegated to a subject the command he should himself assume. Oh, Boabdil," he continued passionately, "friend of my boyhood ere the evil days came upon us, gladly would I sink to rest beneath the dark waves of yonder river if thy arm and brain would fill up my place amongst the warriors of Granada. And think not I say this only from our boyish love; think not I have placed my life in thy hands only from that servile loyalty to a single man which the false chivalry of Christendom imposes as a sacred creed upon its knights and nobles.

But I speak and act but from one principle, — to save the religion of my father and the land of my birth. For this I have risked my life against the foe; for this I surrender my life to the sovereign of my country. Granada may yet survive, if monarch and people unite together; Granada is lost forever if her children at this fatal hour are divided against themselves. If, then, I, O Boabdil, am the true obstacle to thy league with thine own subjects, give me at once to the bowstring, and my sole prayer shall be for the last remnant of the Moorish name, and the last monarch of the Moorish dynasty."

"My son, my son, art thou convinced at last?" cried the queen, struggling with her tears; for she was one who wept easily at heroic sentiments, but never at the softer sorrows or from the more womanly emotions.

Boabdil lifted his head with a vain and momentary attempt at pride; his eye glanced from his mother to his friend, and his better feelings gushed upon him with irresistible force. He threw himself into Muza's arms.

"Forgive me," he said, in broken accents, "forgive me! How could I have wronged thee thus? Yes," he continued, as he started from the noble breast on which for a moment he indulged no ungenerous weakness, — "yes, prince, your example shames, but it fires me. Granada henceforth shall have two chieftains; and if I be jealous of thee, it shall be from an emulation thou canst not blame. Guards, retire. Mesnour! ho, Mesnour! Proclaim at daybreak that I myself will review the troops in the Vivarrambla. Yet," and as he spoke his voice faltered and his brow became overcast, — "yet stay, seek me thyself at daybreak, and I will give thee my commands."

"Oh, my son, why hesitate," cried the queen, "why waver? Prosecute thine own kingly designs, and — "

"Hush, madam," said Boabdil, regaining his customary cold composure; "and since you are now satisfied with your son, leave me alone with Muza."

The queen sighed heavily; but there was something in the calm of Boabdil which chilled and awed her more than his

bursts of passion. She drew her veil around her, and passed
slowly and reluctantly from the chamber.

"Muza," said Boabdil, when alone with the prince, and
fixing his large and thoughtful eyes upon the dark orbs of
his companion, "when, in our younger days, we conversed
together, do you remember how often that converse turned
upon those solemn and mysterious themes to which the sages
of our ancestral land directed their deepest lore, — the
enigmas of the stars, the science of fate, the wild searches
into the clouded future which hides the destinies of nations
and of men? Thou rememberest, Muza, that to such studies
mine own vicissitudes and sorrows, even in childhood, the
strange fortunes which gave me in my cradle the epithet of
El Zogoybi, the ominous predictions of santons and astrologers as to the trials of my earthly fate, — all contributed to
incline my soul. Thou didst not despise those earnest mus-
ings nor our ancestral lore, though, unlike me, ever more
inclined to action than to contemplation, that which thou
mightest believe had little influence upon what thou didst
design. With me it hath been otherwise, — every event of
life hath conspired to feed my early prepossessions; and in
this awful crisis of my fate I have placed myself and my
throne rather under the guardianship of spirits than of men.
This alone has reconciled me to inaction, to the torpor of the
Alhambra, to the mutinies of my people. I have smiled when
foes surrounded and friends deserted me, secure of the aid at
last, — if I bided but the fortunate hour, — of the charms of
protecting spirits and the swords of the invisible creation.
Thou wonderest what this should lead to. Listen! Two
nights since," and the king shuddered, "I was with the dead!
My father appeared before me, not as I knew him in life, —
gaunt and terrible, full of the vigour of health and the
strength of kingly empire and of fierce passion, — but wan,
calm, shadowy. From lips on which Azrael had set his livid
seal he bade me beware of *thee!*"

The king ceased suddenly, and sought to read on the face
of Muza the effect his words produced. But the proud and
swarthy features of the Moor evinced no pang of conscience;

a slight smile of pity might have crossed his lip for a moment, but it vanished ere the king could detect it. Boabdil
continued.

"Under the influence of this warning, I issued the order
for thy arrest. Let this pass, — I resume my tale. I attempted to throw myself at the spectre's feet; it glided from
me, motionless and impalpable. I asked the Dead One if he
forgave his unhappy son the sin of rebellion, — alas! too well
requited even upon earth. And the voice again came forth,
and bade me keep the crown that I had gained, as the sole
atonement for the past. Then again I asked whether the
hour for action had arrived. And the spectre, while it faded
gradually into air, answered, 'No.' 'Oh,' I exclaimed, 'ere
thou leavest me, be one sign accorded me that I have not
dreamed this vision; and give me, I pray thee, note and
warning when the evil star of Boabdil shall withhold its
influence, and he may strike, without resistance from the
Powers above, for his glory and his throne.' 'The sign and
the warning are bequeathed thee,' answered the ghostly image.
It vanished; thick darkness fell around, and when once more
the light of the lamps we bore became visible, behold there
stood before me a skeleton in the regal robe of the kings of
Granada, and on its grisly head was the imperial diadem.
With one hand raised, it pointed to the opposite wall,
wherein burned, like an orb of gloomy fire, a broad dial-
plate, on which were graven these words: 'BEWARE; FEAR
NOT; ARM!' The finger of the dial moved rapidly round, and
rested at the word 'beware.' From that hour to the one in
which I last beheld it, it hath not moved. Muza, the tale is
done. Wilt thou visit with me this enchanted chamber, and
see if the hour be come?"

"Commander of the faithful," said Muza, "the story is
dread and awful. But pardon thy friend, — wert thou alone,
or was the santon Almamen thy companion?"

"Why the question?" said Boabdil, evasively, and slightly
colouring.

"I fear his truth," answered Muza. "The Christian king
conquers more foes by craft than force, and his spies are more

deadly than his warriors. Wherefore this caution against me,
but (pardon me) for thine own undoing? Were I a traitor,
could Ferdinand himself have endangered thy crown so immi-
nently as the revenge of the leader of thine own armies?
Why, too, this desire to keep thee inactive? For the brave
every hour hath its chances; but for us, every hour increases
our peril. If we seize not the present time, our supplies are
cut off, — and famine is a foe all our valour cannot resist.
This dervise, who is he? A stranger, not of our race and
blood. But this morning I found him without the walls, not
far from the Spaniards' camp."

"Ha!" cried the king, quickly, "and what said he?"

"Little, but in hints, — sheltering himself, by loose hints,
under thy name."

"He! What dared he own? Muza, what were those
hints?"

The Moor here recounted the interview with Almamen,
his detention, his inactivity in the battle, and his subsequent
capture by the Spaniards. The king listened attentively,
and regained his composure.

"It is a strange and awful man," said he, after a pause.
"Guards and chains will not detain him. Ere long he will
return. But thou at least, Muza, art henceforth free, alike
from the suspicion of the living and the warnings of the dead.
No, my friend," continued Boabdil, with generous warmth, "it
is better to lose a crown, to lose life itself, than confidence in
a heart like thine. Come, let us inspect this magic tablet;
perchance — and how my heart bounds as I utter the hope! —
the hour may have arrived."

CHAPTER IV.

A FULLER VIEW OF THE CHARACTER OF BOABDIL. — MUZA
IN THE GARDENS OF HIS BELOVED.

MUZA BEN ABIL GAZAN returned from his visit to Boabdil
with a thoughtful and depressed spirit. His arguments had
failed to induce the king to disdain the command of the magic
dial, which still forebade him to arm against the invaders;
and although the royal favour was no longer withdrawn from
himself, the Moor felt that such favour hung upon a capricious and uncertain tenure so long as his sovereign was the
slave of superstition or imposture. But that noble warrior,
whose character the adversity of his country had singularly
exalted and refined, even while increasing its natural fierceness, thought little of himself in comparison with the evils
and misfortunes which the king's continued irresolution must
bring upon Granada.

"So brave, and yet so weak," thought he; "so weak, and
yet so obstinate; so wise a reasoner, yet so credulous a dupe!
Unhappy Boabdil, the stars indeed seem to fight against thee,
and their influences at thy birth marred all thy gifts and virtues with counteracting infirmity and error."

Muza — more, perhaps, than any subject in Granada — did
justice to the real character of the king; but even he was
unable to penetrate all its complicated and latent mysteries.
Boabdil el Chico was no ordinary man. His affections were
warm and generous, his nature calm and gentle; and though
early power and the painful experience of a mutinous people
and ungrateful court had imparted to that nature an irasci-
bility of temper and a quickness of suspicion foreign to its
earlier soil, he was easily led back to generosity and justice;
and if warm in resentment, was magnanimous in forgiveness.
Deeply accomplished in all the learning of his race and time,

he was — in books, at least — a philosopher; and, indeed, his attachment to the abstruser studies was one of the main causes which unfitted him for his present station. But it was the circumstances attendant on his birth and childhood that had perverted his keen and graceful intellect to morbid indulgence in mystic reveries and all the doubt, fear, and irresolution of a man who pushes metaphysics into the supernatural world. Dark prophecies accumulated omens over his head; men united in considering him born to disastrous destinies. Whenever he had sought to wrestle against hostile circumstances, some seemingly accidental cause, sudden and unforeseen, had blasted the labours of his most vigorous energy, the fruit of his most deliberate wisdom. Thus, by degrees a gloomy and despairing cloud settled over his mind; but secretly sceptical of the Mohammedan creed, and too proud and sanguine to resign himself wholly and passively to the doctrine of inevitable predestination, he sought to contend against the machinations of hostile demons and boding stars, not by human, but spiritual agencies. Collecting around him the seers and magicians of Orient-fanaticism, he lived in the visions of another world; and flattered by the promises of impostors or dreamers, and deceived by his own subtle and brooding tendencies of mind, it was amongst spells and cabala that he thought to draw forth the mighty secret which was to free him from the meshes of the preternatural enemies of his fortune, and leave him the freedom of other men to wrestle, with equal chances, against peril and adversities. It was thus that Almamen had won the mastery over his mind; and though upon matters of common and earthly import or solid learning, Boabdil could contend with sages, upon those of superstition he could be fooled by a child. He was in this a kind of Hamlet, formed, under prosperous and serene fortunes, to render blessings and reap renown, but over whom the chilling shadow of another world had fallen, whose soul curdled back into itself, whose life had been separated from that of the herd, whom doubts and awe drew back, while circumstances impelled onward, whom a supernatural doom invested with a peculiar philosophy, not of human effect and cause, and who, with every gift that could ennoble and adorn, was suddenly palsied into that mortal imbecility which is almost ever the result of mortal visitings into the haunted regions of the Ghostly and Unknown. The gloomier colourings of his mind had been deepened, too, by secret remorse. For the preservation of his own life, constantly threatened by his unnatural predecessor, he had been early driven into rebellion against his father. In age, infirmity, and blindness, that fierce king had been made a prisoner at Salobrena by his brother, El Zagal, Boabdil's partner in rebellion; and dying suddenly, El Zagal was suspected of his murder. Though Boabdil was innocent of such a crime, he felt himself guilty of the causes which led to it; and a dark memory, resting upon his conscience, served to augment his superstition and enervate the vigour of his resolves: for of all things that make men dreamers, none is so effectual as remorse operating upon a thoughtful temperament.

Revolving the character of his sovereign, and sadly foreboding the ruin of his country, the young hero of Granada pursued his way until his steps, almost unconsciously, led him towards the abode of Leila. He scaled the walls of the garden as before, he neared the house. All was silent and deserted; his signal was unanswered, his murmured song brought no grateful light to the lattice, no fairy footstep to the balcony. Dejected and sad of heart, he retired from the spot, and returning home, sought a couch, to which even all the fatigue and excitement he had undergone could not win the forgetfulness of slumber. The mystery that wrapped the maiden of his homage, the rareness of their interviews, and the wild and poetical romance that made a very principle of the chivalry of the Spanish Moors, had imparted to Muza's love for Leila a passionate depth which at this day, and in more enervated climes, is unknown to the Mohammedan lover. His keenest inquiries had been unable to pierce the secret of her birth and station. Little of the inmates of that guarded and lonely house was known in the neighbourhood; the only one ever seen without its walls was an old man of the Jewish faith, supposed to be a superintendent of the for-

eign slaves (for no Mohammedan slave would have been subjected to the insult of submission to a Jew); and though there
were rumours of the vast wealth and gorgeous luxury within
the mansion, it was supposed the abode of some Moorish emir
absent from the city, and the interest of the gossips was at
this time absorbed in more weighty matters than the affairs
of a neighbour. But when, the next eve, and the next, Muza
returned to the spot equally in vain, his impatience and alarm
could no longer be restrained; he resolved to lie in watch by
the portals of the house night and day until at least he could
discover some one of the inmates whom he could question of
his love, and perhaps bribe to his service. As with this resolution he was hovering round the mansion, he beheld, stealing
from a small door in one of the low wings of the house, a
bended and decrepit form. It supported its steps upon a
staff; and as, now entering the garden, it stooped by the side
of a fountain to cull flowers and herbs by the light of the
moon, the Moor almost started to behold a countenance which
resembled that of some ghoul or vampire haunting the places
of the dead. He smiled at his own fear, and with a quick
and stealthy pace hastened through the trees, and gaining the
spot where the old man bent, placed his hand on his shoulder
ere his presence was perceived.

Ximen — for it was he — looked round eagerly, and a faint
cry of terror broke from his lips.

"Hush!" said the Moor; "fear me not, I am a friend.
Thou art old, man, — gold is ever welcome to the aged." As
he spoke, he dropped several broad pieces into the breast of
the Jew, whose ghastly features gave forth a yet more ghastly
smile as he received the gift, and mumbled forth, —

"Charitable young man; generous, benevolent, excellent
young man!"

"Now, then," said Muza, "tell me — you belong to this
house — Leila, the maiden within — tell me of her, — is she
well?"

"I trust so," returned the Jew; "I trust so, noble master."

"Trust so! *Know* you not of her state?"

"Not I; for many nights I have not seen her, excellent

sir," answered Ximen, — "she hath left Granada, she hath
gone. You waste your time and mar your precious health
amidst these nightly dews; they are unwholesome, very unwholesome, at the time of the new moon."

"Gone!" echoed the Moor; "left Granada! Woe is me!
And whither? There, there, more gold for you: old man,
tell me whither?"

"Alas! I know not, most magnanimous young man. I am
but a servant; I know nothing."

"When will she return?"

"I cannot tell thee."

"Who is thy master? Who owns yon mansion?"

Ximen's countenance fell; he looked round in doubt and
fear, and then, after a short pause, answered: "A wealthy
man, good sir, — a Moor of Africa; but he hath also gone; he
but seldom visits us: Granada is not so peaceful a residence
as it was. I would go too, if I could."

Muza released his hold of Ximen, who gazed at the Moor's
working countenance with a malignant smile; for Ximen
hated all men.

"Thou hast done with me, young warrior? Pleasant dreams
to thee under the new moon, — thou hadst best retire to thy
bed. Farewell; bless thy charity to the poor old man!"

Muza heard him not; he remained motionless for some
moments, and then with a heavy sigh, as that of one who
has gained the mastery of himself after a bitter struggle, he
said half aloud, "Allah be with thee, Leila! Granada now
is my only mistress."

----◆----

CHAPTER V.

BOABDIL'S RECONCILIATION WITH HIS PEOPLE.

SEVERAL days had elapsed without any encounter between
Moor and Christian; for Ferdinand's cold and sober policy,
warned by the loss he had sustained in the ambush of Muza,

was now bent on preserving rigorous restraint upon the fiery spirits he commanded. He forbade all parties of skirmish, — in which the Moors, indeed, had usually gained the advantage, — and contented himself with occupying all the passes through which provisions could arrive at the besieged city. He commenced strong fortifications around his camp, and forbidding assault on the Moors, defied it against himself.

Meanwhile, Almamen had not returned to Granada. No tidings of his fate reached the king; and his prolonged disappearance began to produce visible and salutary effect upon the long dormant energies of Boabdil. The counsels of Muza, the exhortations of the queen-mother, the enthusiasm of his mistress, Amine, uncounteracted by the arts of the magician, aroused the torpid lion of his nature. But still his army and his subjects murmured against him, and his appearance in the Vivarrambla might possibly be the signal of revolt. It was at this time that a most fortunate circumstance at once restored to him the confidence and affections of his people. His stern uncle, El Zagal, — once a rival for his crown, and whose daring valour, mature age, and military sagacity had won him a powerful party within the city, — had been some months since conquered by Ferdinand; and in yielding the possessions he held, had been rewarded with a barren and dependent principality. His defeat, far from benefiting Boabdil, had exasperated the Moors against their king. "For," said they, almost with one voice, "the brave El Zagal never would have succumbed, had Boabdil properly supported his arms." And it was the popular discontent and rage at El Zagal's defeat which had, indeed, served Boabdil with a reasonable excuse for shutting himself in the strong fortress of the Alhambra. It now happened that El Zagal, whose dominant passion was hatred of his nephew, and whose fierce nature chafed at its present cage, resolved, in his old age, to blast all his former fame by a signal treason to his country. Forgetting everything but revenge against his nephew, who he was resolved should share his own ruin, he armed his subjects, crossed the country, and appeared at the head of a gallant troop in the Spanish camp, an ally with Ferdinand against

K

Granada. When this was heard by the Moors, it is impossible to conceive their indignant wrath. The crime of El Zagal produced an instantaneous reaction in favour of Boabdil; the crowd surrounded the Alhambra, and with prayers and tears entreated the forgiveness of the king. This event completed the conquest of Boabdil over his own irresolution. He ordained an assembly of the whole army in the broad space of the Vivarrambla; and when at break of day he appeared in full armour in the square, with Muza at his right hand, himself in the flower of youthful beauty, and proud to feel once more a hero and a king, the joy of the people knew no limit; the air was rent with cries of "Long live Boabdil el Chico!" and the young monarch, turning to Muza, with his soul upon his brow exclaimed, "The hour has come: I am no longer El Zogoybi!"

CHAPTER VI.

LEILA. — HER NEW LOVER. — PORTRAIT OF THE FIRST INQUIS-
ITOR OF SPAIN. — THE CHALICE RETURNED TO THE LIPS OF
ALMAMEN.

WHILE thus the state of events within Granada, the course of our story transports us back to the Christian camp. It was in one of a long line of tents that skirted the pavilion of Isabel, and was appropriated to the ladies attendant on the royal presence, that a young female sat alone. The dusk of evening already gathered around, and only the outline of her form and features was visible. But even that, imperfectly seen, — the dejected attitude of the form, the drooping head, the hands clasped upon the knees, — might have sufficed to denote the melancholy nature of the revery which the maid indulged.

"Ah," thought she, "to what danger am I exposed! If my father, if my lover, dreamed of the persecution to which their poor Leila is abandoned!"

A few tears, large and bitter, broke from her eyes and stole unheeded down her cheek. At that moment the deep and musical chime of a bell was heard summoning the chiefs of the army to prayer; for Ferdinand invested all his worldly schemes with a religious covering, and to his politic war he sought to give the imposing character of a sacred crusade.

"That sound," thought she, sinking on her knees, "summons the Nazarenes to the presence of their God. It reminds me, a captive by the waters of Babylon, that God is ever with the friendless. Oh, succour and defend me, Thou who didst look of old upon Ruth standing amidst the corn, and didst watch over Thy chosen people in the hungry wilderness and in the stranger's land."

Rapt in her mute and passionate devotions, Leila remained long in her touching posture. The bell had ceased, all without was hushed and still, when the drapery stretched across the opening of the tent was lifted, and a young Spaniard, cloaked from head to foot in a long mantle, stood within the space. He gazed in silence upon the kneeling maiden, nor was it until she rose that he made his presence audible.

"Ah, fairest," said he, then, as he attempted to take her hand, "thou wilt not answer my letters, — see me, then, at thy feet. It is thou who teachest me to kneel."

"You, prince!" said Leila, agitated, and in great and evident fear. "Why harass and insult me thus? Am I not sacred as a hostage and a charge? And are name, honour, peace, and all that woman is taught to hold most dear, to be thus robbed from me under the pretext of a love dishonouring to thee and an insult to myself?"

"Sweet one," answered Don Juan, with a slight laugh, "thou hast learned, within yonder walls, a creed of morals little known to Moorish maidens, if fame belies them not. Suffer me to teach thee easier morality and sounder logic. It is no dishonour to a Christian prince to adore beauty like thine; it is no insult to a maiden hostage if the Infant of Spain proffer her the homage of his heart. But we waste time. Spies and envious tongues and vigilant eyes are around us; and it is not often that I can baffle them as I have done

now. Fairest, hear me!" and this time he succeeded in seizing the hand which vainly struggled against his clasp. "Nay,
why so coy? What can female heart desire that my love cannot shower upon thine? Speak but the word, enchanting
maiden, and I will bear thee from these scenes unseemly to
thy gentle eyes. Amidst the pavilions of princes shalt thou
repose, and amidst gardens of the orange and the rose shalt
thou listen to the vows of thine adorer. Surely in these arms
thou wilt not pine for a barbarous home and a fated city.
And if thy pride, sweet maiden, deafen thee to the voice of
Nature, learn that the haughtiest dames of Spain would bend,
in envious court, to the beloved of their future king. This
night — listen to me — I say, listen — this night I will bear
thee hence. Be but mine, and no matter whether heretic or
infidel, or whatever the priests style thee, neither church nor
king shall tear thee from the bosom of thy lover."

"It is well spoken, son of the most Christian monarch!"
said a deep voice; and the Dominican, Tomas de Torquemada,
stood before the prince.

Juan, as if struck by a thunderbolt, released his hold, and,
staggering back a few paces, seemed to cower, abashed and
humbled, before the eye of the priest as it glared upon him
through the gathering darkness.

"Prince," said the friar, after a pause, "not to thee will
our Holy Church attribute this crime; thy pious heart hath
been betrayed by sorcery. Retire!"

"Father," said the prince, in a tone into which, despite his
awe of that terrible man, THE FIRST GRAND INQUISITOR OF
SPAIN, his libertine spirit involuntarily forced itself, in a half
latent raillery, "sorcery of eyes like those bewitched the wise
son of a more pious sire than even Ferdinand of Arragon."

"He blasphemes," muttered the monk. "Prince, beware!
You know not what you do."

The prince lingered, and then, as if aware that he must yield,
gathered his cloak round him and left the tent without reply.

Pale and trembling, — with fears no less felt, perhaps,
though more vague and perplexed, than those from which she
had just been delivered, — Leila stood before the monk.

"Be seated, daughter of the faithless," said Torquemada; "we would converse with thee. And as thou valuest — I say not thy soul, for, alas! of that precious treasure thou art not conscious — but mark me, woman! as thou prizest the safety of those delicate limbs and that wanton beauty, answer truly what I shall ask thee. The man who brought thee hither, is he in truth thy father?"

"Alas!" answered Leila, almost fainting with terror at this rude and menacing address, "he is, in truth, mine only parent."

"And his faith, his religion?"

"I have never beheld him pray."

"Hem! he never prays, — a noticeable fact. But of what sect, what creed, does he profess himself?"

"I cannot answer thee."

"Nay, there be means that may wring from thee an answer. Maiden, be not so stubborn; speak! Thinkest thou he serves the temple of the Mohammedan?"

"No, oh, no," answered poor Leila, eagerly, deeming that her reply in this, at least, would be acceptable. "He disowns, he scorns, he abhors, the Moorish faith. Even," she added, "with too fierce a zeal."

"Thou dost not share that zeal, then? Well, worships he in secret after the Christian rites?"

Leila hung her head, and answered not.

"I understand thy silence. And in what belief, maiden, wert thou reared beneath his roof?"

"I know not what it is called among men," answered Leila, with firmness, "but it is the faith of the ONE GOD, who protects His chosen and shall avenge their wrongs, — the God who made earth and heaven, and who, in an idolatrous and benighted world, transmitted the knowledge of Himself and His holy laws from age to age through the channel of one solitary people in the plains of Palestine and by the waters of the Hebron."

"And in that faith thou wert trained, maiden, by thy father?" said the Dominican, calmly. "I am satisfied. Rest here in peace; we may meet again soon."

The last words were spoken with a soft and tranquil smile,

—a smile in which glazing eyes and agonizing hearts had often beheld the ghastly omen of the torture and the stake.

On quitting the unfortunate Leila, the monk took his way towards the neighbouring tent of Ferdinand. But ere he reached it, a new thought seemed to strike the holy man; he altered the direction of his steps, and gained one of those little shrines common in Catholic countries, and which had been hastily built of wood, in the centre of a small copse and by the side of a brawling rivulet, towards the back of the king's pavilion. But one solitary sentry, at the entrance of the copse, guarded the consecrated place; and its exceeding loneliness and quiet were a grateful contrast to the animated world of the surrounding camp. The monk entered the shrine, and fell down on his knees before an image of the Virgin, rudely sculptured, indeed, but richly decorated.

"Ah, Holy Mother!" groaned this singular man, "support me in the trial to which I am appointed. Thou knowest that the glory of thy blessed Son is the sole object for which I live and move and have my being; but at times, alas! the spirit is infected with the weakness of the flesh. *Ora pro nobis*, O Mother of mercy! Verily, oftentimes my heart sinks within me when it is mine to vindicate the honour of thy holy cause against the young and the tender, the aged and the decrepit. But what are beauty and youth, gray hairs and trembling knees, in the eye of the Creator? Miserable worms are we all; nor is there anything acceptable in the Divine sight but the hearts of the faithful. Youth without faith, age without belief, purity without grace, virtue without holiness, are only more hideous by their seeming beauty, — whited sepulchres, glittering rottenness. I know this, I know it, but the human man is strong within me. Strengthen me, that I pluck it out; so that, by diligent and constant struggle with the feeble Adam, thy servant may be reduced into a mere machine to punish the godless and advance the Church."

Here sobs and tears choked the speech of the Dominican; he grovelled in the dust, he tore his hair, he howled aloud: the agony was fierce upon him. At length he drew from his robe a whip composed of several thongs studded with small and sharp nails; and stripping his gown and the shirt of hair worn underneath, over his shoulders, applied the scourge to the naked flesh with a fury which soon covered the green-sward with the thick and clotted blood. The exhaustion which followed this terrible penance seemed to restore the senses of the stern fanatic. A smile broke over the features, that bodily pain only released from the anguished expression of mental and visionary struggles; and when he rose, and drew the hair-cloth shirt over the lacerated and quivering flesh, he said: "Now hast thou deigned to comfort and visit me, O pitying Mother; and even as by these austerities against this miserable body is the spirit relieved and soothed, so dost thou typify and betoken that men's bodies are not to be spared by those who seek to save souls and bring the nations of the earth into thy fold."

With that thought the countenance of Torquemada re-assumed its wonted rigid and passionless composure; and replacing the scourge, yet clotted with blood, in his bosom, he pursued his way to the royal tent.

He found Ferdinand poring over the accounts of the vast expenses of his military preparations, which he had just received from his treasurer; and the brow of the thrifty, though ostentatious monarch, was greatly overcast by the examination.

"By the Bulls of Guisando," said the king, gravely, "I purchase the salvation of my army in this holy war at a mar-vellous heavy price; and if the infidels hold out much longer, we shalt have to pawn our very patrimony of Arragon."

"Son," answered the Dominican, "to purposes like thine, fear not that Providence itself will supply the worldly means. But why doubtest thou? Are not the means within thy reach? It is just that thou alone shouldst not support the wars by which Christendom is glorified. Are there not others?"

"I know what thou wouldst say, father," interrupted the king, quickly, — "thou wouldst observe that my brother mon-archs should assist me with arms and treasure. Most just. But they are avaricious and envious, Tomas, and Mammon hath corrupted them."

"Nay, not to kings pointed my thought."

"Well, then," resumed the king, impatiently, "thou wouldst imply that mine own knights and nobles should yield up their coffers and mortgage their possessions. And so they ought; but they murmur already at what they have yielded to our necessities."

"And in truth," rejoined the friar, "these noble warriors should not be shorn of a splendour that well becomes the valiant champions of the Church. Nay, listen to me, son, and I may suggest a means whereby, not the friends, but enemies, of the Catholic faith shall contribute to the downfall of the Paynim. In thy dominions, especially those newly won, throughout Andalusia, in the kingdom of Cordova, are men of enormous wealth; the very caverns of the earth are sown with the impious treasure they have plundered from Christian hands, and consume in the furtherance of their iniquity. Sire, I speak of the race that crucified the Lord."

"The Jews — ay; but the excuse — "

"Is before thee. This traitor with whom thou holdest intercourse, who vowed to thee to render up Granada, and who was found the very next morning fighting with the Moors, with the blood of a Spanish martyr red upon his hands, did he not confess that his fathers were of that hateful race? Did he not bargain with thee to elevate his brethren to the rank of Christians? And has he not left with thee, upon false pretences, a harlot of his faith, who, by sorcery and the help of the Evil One, hath seduced into frantic passion the heart of the heir of the most Christian king?"

"Ha, thus does that libertine boy ever scandalize us!" said the king, bitterly.

"Well," pursued the Dominican, not heeding the interruption, "have you not here excuse enough to wring from the whole race the purchase of their existence? Note the glaring proof of this conspiracy of hell. The outcasts of the earth employed this crafty agent to contract with thee for power; and, to consummate their guilty designs, the arts that seduced Solomon are employed against thy son. The beauty of the strange woman captivates his senses, so that through the future sovereign of Spain the counsels of Jewish craft may establish the domination of Jewish ambition. How knowest thou," he added, as he observed that Ferdinand listened to him with earnest attention, — "how knowest thou but what the next step might have been thy secret assassination, so that the victim of witchcraft, the minion of the Jewess, might reign in the stead of the mighty and unconquerable Ferdinand?"

"Go on, father," said the king, thoughtfully; "I see at least enough to justify an impost upon these servitors of Mammon."

"But though common-sense suggests to us," continued Torquemada, "that this disguised Israelite could not have acted on so vast a design without the instigation of his brethren, not only in Granada, but throughout all Andalusia, would it not be right to obtain from him his confession, and that of the maiden, within the camp, so that we may have broad and undeniable evidence whereon to act, and to still all cavil, that may come not only from the godless, but even from the too tender scruples of the righteous? Even the queen — whom the saints ever guard! — hath ever too soft a heart for these infidels, and — "

"Right," cried the king, again breaking upon Torquemada; "Isabel, the queen of Castile, must be satisfied of the justice of all our actions."

"And should it be proved that thy throne or life were endangered, and that magic was exercised to entrap her royal son into a passion for a Jewish maiden which the Church holds a crime worthy of excommunication itself, — surely, instead of counteracting, she would assist our schemes."

"Holy friend," said Ferdinand, with energy, "ever a comforter both for this world and the next, to thee and to the new powers intrusted to thee we commit this charge, — see to it at once: time presses; Granada is obstinate; the treasury waxes low."

"Son, thou hast said enough," replied the Dominican, closing his eyes and muttering a short thanksgiving. "Now then to my task."

"Yet stay," said the king, with an altered visage, "follow me to my oratory within. My heart is heavy, and I would fain seek the solace of the confessional."

The monk obeyed; and while Ferdinand, whose wonderful abilities were mingled with the weakest superstition, who persecuted from policy, yet believed, in his own heart, that he punished but from piety, confessed with penitent tears the grave offences of *aves* forgotten and beads untold, and while the Dominican admonished, rebuked, or soothed, — neither prince nor monk ever dreamed that there was an error to confess in, or a penance to be adjudged to, the cruelty that tortured a fellow-being, or the avarice that sought pretences for the extortion of a whole people.

CHAPTER VII.

THE TRIBUNAL AND THE MIRACLE.

It was the dead of night, the army was hushed in sleep, when four soldiers belonging to the Holy Brotherhood, bearing with them one whose manacles proclaimed him a prisoner, passed in steady silence to a huge tent in the neighbourhood of the royal pavilion. A deep dike, formidable barricadoes, and sentries stationed at frequent intervals, testified the estimation in which the safety of this segment of the camp was held. The tent to which the soldiers approached was in extent larger than even the king's pavilion itself, — a mansion of canvas, surrounded by a wide wall of massive stones; and from its summit gloomed, in the clear and shining starlight, a small black pennant, on which was wrought a white broad-pointed cross. The soldiers halted at the gate in the wall, resigned their charge, with a whispered watchword, to two gaunt sentries; and then (relieving the sentries, who proceeded on with the prisoner) remained, mute and motionless, at the post: for stern silence and Spartan discipline were the attributes of the brotherhood of St. Hermandad.

The prisoner, as he now neared the tent, halted a moment, looked round steadily, as if to fix the spot in his remembrance, and then, with an impatient though stately gesture, followed his guards. He passed two divisions of the tent, dimly lighted, and apparently deserted. A man clad in long black robes, with a white cross on his breast, now appeared; there was an interchange of signals in dumb-show, and in another moment Almamen the Hebrew stood within a large chamber (if so that division of the tent might be called) hung with black serge. At the upper part of the space was an *estrado*, or platform, on which, by a long table, sat three men, while at the head of the board was seen the calm and rigid countenance of Tomas de Torquemada. The threshold of the tent was guarded by two men in garments similar in hue and fashion to those of the figure who had ushered Almamen into the presence of the inquisitor, each bearing a long lance, and with a long two-edged sword by his side. This made all the inhabitants of that melancholy and ominous apartment.

The Israelite looked round with a pale brow, but a flashing and scornful eye; and when he met the gaze of the Dominican, it almost seemed as if those two men, each so raised above his fellows by the sternness of his nature and the energy of his passions, sought by a look alone to assert his own supremacy and crush his foe. Yet in truth neither did justice to the other, and the indignant disdain of Almamen was retorted by the cold and icy contempt of the Dominican.

"Prisoner," said Torquemada (the first to withdraw his gaze), "a less haughty and stubborn demeanour might have better suited thy condition. But no matter; our Church is meek and humble. We have sent for thee in a charitable and paternal hope; for although as spy and traitor thy life is already forfeited, yet would we fain redeem and spare it to repentance. That hope mayst thou not forego, for the nature of all of us is weak and clings to life, — that straw of the drowning seaman."

"Priest, if such thou art," replied the Hebrew, "I have already, when first brought to this camp, explained the causes of my detention amongst the troops of the Moor. It was my zeal for the king of Spain that brought me into that peril. Escaping from that peril, incurred in his behalf, is the king of Spain to be my accuser and my judge? If, however, my life now be sought as the grateful return for the proffer of inestimable service, I stand here to yield it. Do thy worst; and tell thy master that he loses more by my death than he can win by the lives of thirty thousand warriors."

"Cease this idle babble," said the monk-inquisitor, contemptuously, "nor think thou couldst ever deceive, with thy empty words, the mighty intellect of Ferdinand of Spain. Thou hast now to defend thyself against still graver charges than those of treachery to the king whom thou didst profess to serve. Yea, misbeliever as thou art, it is thine to vindicate thyself from blasphemy against the God thou shouldst adore. Confess the truth: thou art of the tribe and faith of Israel?"

The Hebrew frowned darkly. "Man," said he, solemnly, "is a judge of the deeds of men, but not of their opinions. I will not answer thee."

"Pause! We have means at hand that the strongest nerves and the stoutest hearts have failed to encounter. Pause, — confess!"

"Thy threat awes me not," said the Hebrew, "but I am human; and since thou wouldst know the truth, thou mayst learn it without the torture. I am of the same race as the apostles of thy Church, — I am a Jew."

"He confesses, — write down the words. Prisoner, thou hast done wisely; and we pray the Lord that, acting thus, thou mayst escape both the torture and the death. And in that faith thy daughter was reared? Answer."

"My daughter! there is no charge against her! By the God of Sinai and Horeb, you dare not touch a hair of that innocent head!"

"Answer," repeated the inquisitor, coldly.

"I do answer. She was brought up no renegade to her father's faith."

"Write down the confession. Prisoner," resumed the

Dominican, after a pause, "but few more questions remain; answer them truly, and thy life is saved. In thy conspiracy to raise thy brotherhood of Andalusia to power and influence, or, as thou didst craftily term it, to equal laws with the followers of our blessed Lord, — in thy conspiracy (by what dark arts I seek not now to know; *protege nos, beate Domine!*) to entangle in wanton affections to thy daughter the heart of the Infant of Spain, — silence, I say; be still! — in this conspiracy, thou wert aided, abetted, or instigated by certain Jews of Andalusia — "

"Hold, priest!" cried Almamen, impetuously; "thou didst name my child. Do I hear aright? Placed under the sacred charge of a king and a belted knight, has she — oh, answer me, I implore thee — been insulted by the licentious addresses of one of that king's own lineage? Answer! I am a Jew, but I am a father and a man."

"This pretended passion deceives us not," said the Dominican, who, himself cut off from the ties of life, knew nothing of their power. "Reply to the question put to thee: name thy accomplices."

"I have told thee all. Thou hast refused to answer *me*. I scorn and defy thee; my lips are closed."

The Grand Inquisitor glanced to his brethren and raised his hand. His assistants whispered each other; one of them rose, and disappeared behind the canvas at the back of the tent. Presently the hangings were withdrawn, and the prisoner beheld an interior chamber, hung with various instruments the nature of which was betrayed by their very shape; while by the rack, placed in the centre of that dreary chamber, stood a tall and grisly figure, his arms bare, his eyes bent as by an instinct on the prisoner.

Almamen gazed at these dread preparations with an unflinching aspect. The guards at the entrance of the tent approached; they struck off the fetters from his feet and hands; they led him towards the appointed place of torture.

Suddenly the Israelite paused.

"Priest," said he, in a more humble accent than he had yet assumed, "the tidings that thou didst communicate to me respecting the sole daughter of my house and love bewildered and confused me for the moment. Suffer me but for a single moment to re-collect my senses, and I will answer without compulsion all thou mayst ask. Permit thy questions to be repeated."

The Dominican, whose cruelty to others seemed to himself sanctioned by his own insensibility to fear and contempt for bodily pain, smiled with bitter scorn at the apparent vacillation and weakness of the prisoner; but as he delighted not in torture merely for torture's sake, he motioned to the guards to release the Israelite, and replied, in a voice unnaturally mild and kindly, considering the circumstances of the scene, —

"Prisoner, could we save thee from pain, even by the anguish of our own flesh and sinews, Heaven is our judge that we would willingly undergo the torture which, with grief and sorrow, we ordained to thee. Pause, take breath, collect thyself. Three minutes shalt thou have to consider what course to adopt ere we repeat the question; but then beware how thou triflest with our indulgence."

"It suffices, I thank thee," said the Hebrew, with a touch of gratitude in his voice. As he spoke, he bent his face within his bosom, which he covered, as in profound meditation, with the folds of his long robe. Scarce half the brief time allowed him had expired, when he again lifted his countenance, and as he did so, flung back his garment. The Dominican uttered a loud cry; the guards started back in awe. A wonderful change had come over the intended victim: he seemed to stand amongst them literally wrapped in fire; flames burst from his lip and played with his long locks, as, catching the glowing hue, they curled over his shoulders like serpents of burning light; blood-red were his breast and limbs, his haughty crest, and his outstretched arm; and as for a single moment he met the shuddering eyes of his judges, he seemed, indeed, to verify all the superstitions of the time, — no longer the trembling captive, but the mighty demon or the terrible magician.

The Dominican was the first to recover his self-possession.

"Seize the enchanter!" he exclaimed; but no man stirred. Ere yet the exclamation had died on his lip, Almamen took from his breast a phial and dashed it on the ground, — it broke into a thousand shivers; a mist rose over the apartment; it spread, thickened, darkened, as a sudden night; the lamps could not pierce it. The luminous form of the Hebrew grew dull and dim, until it vanished in the shade. On every eye blindness seemed to fall. There was a dead silence, broken by a cry and a groan; and when, after some minutes, the darkness gradually dispersed, Almamen was gone. One of the guards lay bathed in blood upon the ground; they raised him: he had attempted to seize the prisoner, and had been stricken with a mortal wound. He died as he faltered forth the explanation. In the confusion and dismay of the scene, none noticed, till long afterwards, that the prisoner had paused long enough to strip the dying guard of his long mantle, — a proof that he feared his more secret arts might not suffice to bear him safe through the camp without the aid of worldly stratagem.

"The fiend hath been amongst us," said the Dominican, solemnly falling on his knees; "let us pray!"

BOOK III.

CHAPTER I.

ISABEL AND THE JEWISH MAIDEN.

WHILE this scene took place before the tribunal of Torque-mada, Leila had been summoned from the indulgence of fears, which her gentle nature and her luxurious nurturing had ill fitted her to contend against, to the presence of the queen. That gifted and high-spirited princess, whose virtues were her own, whose faults were of her age, was not, it is true, without the superstition and something of the intolerant spirit of her royal spouse; but even where her faith assented to persecution, her heart ever inclined to mercy, and it was her voice alone that ever counteracted the fiery zeal of Torquemada, and mitigated the sufferings of the unhappy ones who fell under the suspicion of heresy. She had, hap-pily, too, within her a strong sense of justice, as well as the sentiment of compassion; and often, when she could not save the accused, she prevented the consequences of his imputed crime falling upon the innocent members of his house or tribe.

In the interval between his conversation with Ferdinand and the examination of Almamen, the Dominican had sought the queen, and had placed before her in glowing colours, not only the treason of Almamen, but the consequences of the impious passion her son had conceived for Leila. In that day, any connection between a Christian knight and a Jewess was deemed a sin scarce expiable; and Isabel conceived all that horror of her son's offence which was natural in a pious mother and a haughty queen. But despite all the arguments of the friar, she could not be prevailed upon to render up

Leila to the tribunal of the Inquisition; and that dread court, but newly established, did not dare, without her consent, to seize upon one under the immediate protection of the queen.

"Fear not, father," said Isabel, with quiet firmness, "I will take upon myself to examine the maiden; and at least I will see her removed from all chance of tempting or being tempted by this graceless boy. But she was placed under the charge of the king and myself as a hostage and a trust; we accepted the charge, and our royal honour is pledged to the safety of the maiden. Heaven forbid that I should deny the existence of sorcery, assured as we are of its emanation from the Evil One; but I fear, in this fancy of Juan's, that the maiden is more sinned against than sinning. And yet my son is doubtless not aware of the unhappy faith of the Jewess, the knowledge of which alone will suffice to cure him of his error. You shake your head, father; but, I repeat, I will act in this affair so as to merit the confidence I demand. Go, good Tomas. We have not reigned so long without belief in our power to control and deal with a simple maiden."

The queen extended her hand to the monk with a smile so sweet in its dignity that it softened even that rugged heart; and with a reluctant sigh and a murmured prayer that her counsels might be guided for the best, Torquemada left the royal presence.

"The poor child!" thought Isabel; "those tender limbs and that fragile form are ill fitted for yon monk's stern tutelage. She seems gentle, and her face has in it all the yielding softness of our sex. Doubtless by mild means she may be persuaded to abjure her wretched creed; and the shade of some holy convent may hide her alike from the licentious gaze of my son and the iron zeal of the Inquisitor. I will see her."

When Leila entered the queen's pavilion, Isabel, who was alone, marked her trembling step with a compassionate eye; and as Leila, in obedience to the queen's request, threw up her veil, the paleness of her cheek and the traces of recent tears appealed to Isabel's heart with more success than had attended all the pious invectives of Torquemada.

6

"Maiden," said Isabel, encouragingly, "I fear thou hast been strangely harassed by the thoughtless caprice of the young prince. Think of it no more. But if thou art what I have ventured to believe and to assert thee to be, cheerfully subscribe to the means I will suggest for preventing the continuance of addresses which cannot but injure thy fair name."

"Ah, madam!" said Leila, as she fell on one knee beside the queen, "most joyfully, most gratefully, will I accept any asylum which proffers solitude and peace."

"The asylum to which I would fain lead thy steps," answered Isabel, gently, "is indeed one whose solitude is holy, whose peace is that of Heaven. But of this hereafter. Thou wilt not hesitate, then, to quit the camp, unknown to the prince, and ere he can again seek thee?"

"Hesitate, madam? Ah! rather, how shall I express my thanks?"

"I did not read that face misjudgingly," thought the queen as she resumed. "Be it so; we will not lose another night. Withdraw yonder, through the inner tent; the litter shall be straight prepared for thee, and ere midnight thou shalt sleep in safety under the roof of one of the bravest knights and noblest ladies that our realm can boast. Thou shalt bear with thee a letter that shall commend thee specially to the care of thy hostess; thou wilt find her of a kindly and fostering nature. And oh, maiden!" added the queen, with benevolent warmth, "steel not thy heart against her, listen with ductile senses to her gentle ministry. And may God and His Son prosper that pious lady's counsel, so that it may win a new strayling to the Immortal Fold!"

Leila listened and wondered, but made no answer, until, as she gained the entrance to the interior division of the tent, she stopped abruptly, and said, —

"Pardon me, gracious queen, but dare I ask thee one question? It is not of myself."

"Speak, and fear not."

"My father, hath aught been heard of him? He promised that ere the fifth day were past he would once more see his child; and alas! that date is past, and I am still alone in the dwelling of the stranger."

"Unhappy child," muttered Isabel to herself, "thou knowest not his treason nor his fate. Yet why shouldst thou? Ignorant of what would render thee blest hereafter, continue ignorant of what would afflict thee here. Be cheered, maiden," answered the queen, aloud. "No doubt there are reasons sufficient to forbid your meeting. But thou shalt not lack friends in the dwelling-house of the stranger."

"Ah, noble queen, pardon me, and one word more. There hath been with me, more than once, a stern old man, whose voice freezes the blood within my veins; he questions me of my father, and in the tone of a foe who would entrap from the child something to the peril of the sire. That man, — thou knowest him, gracious queen, — he cannot have the power to harm my father?"

"Peace, maiden! The man thou speakest of is the priest of God, and the innocent have nothing to dread from his reverend zeal. For thyself, I say again, be cheered; in the home to which I consign thee thou wilt see him no more. Take comfort, poor child; weep not. All have their cares; our duty is to bear in this life, reserving hope only for the next."

The queen, destined herself to those domestic afflictions which pomp cannot soothe, nor power allay, spoke with a prophetic sadness which yet more touched a heart that her kindness of look and tone had already softened; and in the impulse of a nature never tutored in the rigid ceremonials of that stately court, Leila suddenly came forward, and falling on one knee, seized the hand of her protectress and kissed it warmly through her tears.

"Are you, too, unhappy?" she said. "I will pray for you to *my* God!"

The queen, surprised and moved at an action which, had witnesses been present, would only perhaps (for such is human nature) have offended her Castilian prejudices, left her hand in Leila's grateful clasp; and laying the other upon the parted and luxuriant ringlets of the kneeling maiden, said gently: "And thy prayers shall avail thee and me when thy God and mine are the same. Bless thee, maiden! I am a mother; thou art motherless, — bless thee!"

CHAPTER II.

THE TEMPTATION OF THE JEWESS. — IN WHICH THE HISTORY PASSES FROM THE OUTWARD TO THE INTERNAL.

IT was about the very hour, almost the very moment, in which Almamen effected his mysterious escape from the tent of the Inquisition that the train accompanying the litter which bore Leila, and which was composed of some chosen soldiers of Isabel's own body-guard, after traversing the camp, winding along that part of the mountainous defile which was in the possession of the Spaniards, and ascending a high and steep acclivity, halted before the gates of a strongly fortified castle, renowned in the chronicles of that memorable war. The hoarse challenge of the sentry, the grating of jealous bars, the clanks of hoofs upon the rough pavement of the courts, and the streaming glare of torches, — falling upon stern and bearded visages, and imparting a ruddier glow to the moonlit buttresses and battlements of the fortress, — aroused Leila from a kind of torpor rather than sleep, in which the fatigue and excitement of the day had steeped her senses. An old seneschal conducted her through vast and gloomy halls (how unlike the brilliant chambers and fantastic arcades of her Moorish home!) to a huge Gothic apartment, hung with the arras of Flemish looms. In a few moments maidens, hastily aroused from slumber, grouped around her with a respect which would certainly not have been accorded had her birth and creed been known. They gazed with surprise at her extraordinary beauty and foreign garb, and evidently considered the new guest a welcome addition to the scanty society of the castle. Under any other circumstances, the strangeness of all she saw, and the frowning gloom of the chamber to which she was consigned, would have damped the spirits of one whose destiny had so suddenly passed from the deepest quiet into the sternest excitement. But any change was a relief to the roar of the camp, the addresses of the prince, and the ominous voice and countenance of Torquemada; and Leila looked around her with the feeling that the queen's promise was fulfilled, and that she was already amidst the blessings of shelter and repose. It was long, however, before sleep revisited her eyelids, and when she woke, the noonday sun streamed broadly through the lattice. By the bedside sat a matron advanced in years, but of a mild and prepossessing countenance, which only borrowed a yet more attractive charm from an expression of placid and habitual melancholy. She was robed in black; but the rich pearls that were interwoven in the sleeves and stomacher, the jewelled cross that was appended from a chain of massive gold, and, still more, a certain air of dignity and command, bespoke, even to the inexperienced eye of Leila, the evidence of superior station.

"Thou hast slept late, daughter," said the lady, with a benevolent smile; "may thy slumbers have refreshed thee! Accept my regrets that I knew not till this morning of thine arrival, or I should have been the first to welcome the charge of my royal mistress."

There was in the look, much more than in the words of the Donna Inez de Quexada, a soothing and tender interest that was as balm to the heart of Leila; in truth, she had been made the guest of perhaps the only lady in Spain, of pure and Christian blood, who did not despise or execrate the name of Leila's tribe. Donna Inez had herself contracted to a Jew a debt of gratitude which she had sought to return to the whole race. Many years before the time in which our tale is cast, her husband and herself had been sojourning at Naples, then closely connected with the politics of Spain, upon an important State mission. They had then an only son, a youth of a wild and desultory character, whom the spirit of adventure allured to the East. In one of those sultry lands the young

Quexada was saved from the hands of robbers by the caravan-
serai of a wealthy traveller. With this stranger he contracted
that intimacy which wandering and romantic men often conceive for each other, without any other sympathy than that
of the same pursuits. Subsequently, he discovered that his
companion was of the Jewish faith, and with the usual preju-
dice of his birth and time, recoiled from the friendship he had
solicited, and shrank from the sense of the obligation he
had incurred: he quitted his companion. Wearied, at length,
with travel, he was journeying homeward when he was seized
with a sudden and virulent fever, mistaken for plague; all
fled from the contagion of the supposed pestilence, — he was
left to die. One man discovered his condition, — watched,
tended, and, skilled in the deeper secrets of the healing art,
restored him to life and health: it was the same Jew who
had preserved him from the robbers. At this second and
more inestimable obligation the prejudices of the Spaniard
vanished; he formed a deep and grateful attachment for his
preserver. They lived together for some time, and the Israelite finally accompanied the young Quexada to Naples. Inez
retained a lively sense of the service rendered to her only son,
and the impression had been increased, not only by the appearance of the Israelite, which, dignified and stately, bore
no likeness to the cringing servility of his brethren, but also
by the singular beauty and gentle deportment of his then
newly wed bride, whom he had wooed and won in that holy
land sacred equally to the faith of Christian and of Jew.
The young Quexada did not long survive his return; his con-
stitution was broken by long travel and the debility that followed his fierce disease. On his deathbed he had besought
the mother whom he left childless, and whose Catholic prejudices were less stubborn than those of his sire, never to forget
the services a Jew had conferred upon him, to make the sole
recompense in her power, — the sole recompense the Jew himself had demanded, — and to lose no occasion to soothe or
mitigate the miseries to which the bigotry of the time often
exposed the oppressed race of his deliverer. Donna Inez had
faithfully kept the promise she gave to the last scion of her

house, and through the power and reputation of her husband
and her own connections, and still more through an early
friendship with the queen, she had, on her return to Spain,
been enabled to ward off many a persecution, and many a
charge on false pretences, to which the wealth of some son of
Israel made the cause, while his faith made the pretext. Yet,
with all the natural feelings of a rigid Catholic, she had earnestly sought to render the favour she had thus obtained
amongst the Jews minister to her pious zeal for their more
than temporal welfare. She had endeavoured by gentle
means to make the conversions which force was impotent
to effect; and in some instances her success had been signal.
The good señora had thus obtained high renown for sanctity;
and Isabel thought rightly that she could not select a protectress for Leila who would more kindly shelter her youth, or
more strenuously labour for her salvation. It was, indeed, a
dangerous situation for the adherence of the maiden to that
faith which it had cost her fiery father so many sacrifices to
preserve and to advance.

It was by little and little that Donna Inez sought rather to
undermine than to storm the mental fortress she hoped to
man with spiritual allies; and in her frequent conversations
with Leila she was at once perplexed and astonished by the
simple and sublime nature of the belief upon which she waged
war. For whether it was that, in his desire to preserve Leila
as much as possible from contact even with Jews themselves,
whose general character (vitiated by the oppression which
engendered meanness, and the extortion which fostered avarice) Almamen regarded with lofty though concealed repug-
nance, or whether it was that his philosophy did not interpret
the Jewish formula of belief in the same spirit as the herd,
— the religion inculcated in the breast of Leila was different
from that which Inez had ever before encountered amongst
her proselytes. It was less mundane and material, — a kind
of passionate rather than metaphysical theism, which invested
the great ONE, indeed, with many human sympathies and
attributes, but still left Him the august and awful God of the
Genesis, the Father of a Universe, though the individual

Protector of a fallen sect. Her attention had been less
directed to whatever appears, to a superficial gaze, stern and
inexorable in the character of the Hebrew God, and which the
religion of Christ so beautifully softened and so majestically
refined, than to those passages in which His love watched
over a chosen people, and His forbearance bore with their
transgressions. Her reason had been worked upon to its
belief by that mysterious and solemn agency by which —
when the whole world beside was bowed to the worship of
innumerable deities and the adoration of graven images — in
a small and secluded portion of earth, amongst a people far
less civilized and philosophical than many by which they
were surrounded, had been alone preserved a pure and sublime theism, disdaining a likeness in the things of heaven
or earth. Leila knew little of the more narrow and exclusive
tenets of her brethren; a Jewess in name, she was rather a
deist in belief, — a deist of such a creed as Athenian schools
might have taught to the imaginative pupils of Plato, save
only that too dark a shadow had been cast over the hopes of
another world. Without the absolute denial of the Sadducee,
Almamen had probably much of the quiet scepticism which
belonged to many sects of the early Jews, and which still
clings round the wisdom of the wisest who reject the doctrine of Revelation; and while he had not sought to eradicate
from the breast of his daughter any of the vague desire which
points to a Hereafter, he had never, at least, directed her
thoughts or aspirations to that solemn future. Nor in the
sacred book which was given to her survey, and which so
rigidly upheld the unity of the Supreme Power, was there
that positive and unequivocal assurance of life beyond "the
grave where all things are forgotten" that might supply the
deficiencies of her mortal instructor. Perhaps, sharing those
notions of the different value of the sexes, prevalent, from the
remotest period, in his beloved and ancestral East, Almamen
might have hopes for himself which did not extend to his
child. And thus she grew up, with all the beautiful faculties
of the soul cherished and unfolded, without thought, without
more than dim and shadowy conjectures, of the Eternal

Bourn to which the sorrowing pilgrim of the earth is bound. It was on this point that the quick eye of Donna Inez discovered her faith was vulnerable: who would not, if belief were voluntary, believe in the world to come? Leila's curiosity and interest were aroused; she willingly listened to her new guide, she willingly inclined to conclusions pressed upon her, not with menace, but persuasion. Free from the stubborn associations, the sectarian prejudices, and unversed in the peculiar traditions and accounts of the learned of her race, she found nothing to shock her in the volume which seemed but a continuation of the elder writings of her faith. The sufferings of the Messiah, His sublime purity, His meek forgiveness, spoke to her woman's heart; His doctrines elevated, while they charmed, her reason; and in the heaven that a Divine hand opened to all, — the humble as the proud, the oppressed as the oppressor, to the woman as to the lords of the earth, — she found a haven for all the doubts she had known, and for the despair which of late had darkened the face of earth. Her home lost, the deep and beautiful love of her youth blighted, — that was a creed almost irresistible which told her that grief was but for a day, that happiness was eternal. Far, too, from revolting such of the Hebrew pride of association as she had formed, the birth of the Messiah in the land of the Israelites seemed to consummate their peculiar triumph as the Elected of Jehovah. And while she mourned for the Jews who persecuted the Saviour, she gloried in those whose belief had carried the name and worship of the descendants of David over the farthest regions of the world. Often she perplexed and startled the worthy Inez by exclaiming, "This your belief is the same as mine, adding only the assurance of immortal life: Christianity is but the Revelation of Judaism."

The wise and gentle instrument of Leila's conversion did not, however, give vent to those more Catholic sentiments which might have scared away the wings of the descending dove. She forbore too vehemently to point out the distinctions of the several creeds, and rather suffered them to melt insensibly one into the other: Leila was a Christian while she still believed herself a Jewess. But in the fond and lovely weakness of mortal emotions, there was one bitter thought that often and often came to mar the peace that otherwise would have settled on her soul. That father, the sole softener of whose stern heart and mysterious fate she was, with what pangs would he receive the news of her conversion! And Muza, that bright and hero-vision of her youth, — was she not setting the last seal of separation upon all hope of union with the idol of the Moors? But alas! was she not already separated from him, and had not their faiths been from the first at variance? From these thoughts she started with sighs and tears; and before her stood the crucifix already admitted into her chamber, and — not, perhaps, too wisely — banished so rigidly from the oratories of the Huguenot. For the representation of that Divine resignation, that mortal agony, that miraculous sacrifice, what eloquence it hath for our sorrows! What preaching hath the symbol to the van ities of our wishes, to the yearnings of our discontent!

By degrees, as her new faith grew confirmed, Leila now inclined herself earnestly to those pictures of the sanctity and calm of the conventual life which Inez delighted to draw. In the reaction of her thoughts, and her despondency of all worldly happiness, there seemed to the young maiden an inexpressible charm in a solitude which was to release her forever from human love, and render her entirely up to sacred visions and imperishable hopes. And with this selfish, there mingled a generous and sublime sentiment. The prayers of a convent might be heard in favour of those yet benighted, and the awful curse upon her outcast race be lightened by the orisons of one humble heart. In all ages, in all creeds, a strange and mystic impression has existed of the efficacy of self-sacrifice in working the redemption even of a whole people; this belief, so strong in the old Orient and classic religions, was yet more confirmed by Christianity, — a creed founded upon the grand-est of historic sacrifices, and the lofty doctrine of which, rightly understood, perpetuates in the heart of every believer the duty of self-immolation, as well as faith in the power of prayer, no matter how great the object, how mean the supplicator. On these thoughts Leila meditated till thoughts acquired the intensity of passions, and the conversion of the Jewess was completed.

CHAPTER III.

THE HOUR AND THE MAN.

It was on the third morning after the king of Granada, reconciled to his people, had reviewed his gallant army in the Vivarrambla, and Boabdil, surrounded by his chiefs and nobles, was planning a deliberate and decisive battle, by assault on the Christian camp, when a scout suddenly arrived, breathless, at the gates of the palace, to communicate the unlooked-for and welcome intelligence that Ferdinand had in the night broken up his camp and marched across the mountains towards Cordova. In fact, the outbreak of formidable conspiracies had suddenly rendered the appearance of Ferdinand necessary elsewhere; and his intrigues with Almamen frustrated, he despaired of a very speedy conquest of the city. The Spanish king resolved, therefore, after completing the devastation of the Vega, to defer the formal and prolonged siege, which could alone place Granada within his power, until his attention was no longer distracted by other foes, and until, it must be added, he had replenished an exhausted treasury. He had formed, with Torquemada, a vast and wide scheme of persecution, not only against Jews, but against Christians whose fathers had been of that race, and who were suspected of relapsing into Judaical practices. The two schemers of this grand design were actuated by different motives: the one wished to exterminate the crime, the other to sell forgiveness for it. And Torquemada connived at the griping avarice of the king because it served to give to himself and to the infant Inquisition a power and authority which the Dominican foresaw would be soon greater even than those of royalty itself, and which, he imagined, by scourging earth, would redound to the interests of heaven.

The strange disappearance of Almamen, which was distorted and exaggerated by the credulity of the Spaniards into an event of the most terrific character, served to complete the chain of evidence against the wealthy Jews and Jew-descended Spaniards of Andalusia; and while, in imagination, the king already clutched the gold of their redemption here, the Dominican kindled the flame that was to light them to punishment hereafter.

Boabdil and his chiefs received the intelligence of the Spanish retreat with a doubt which soon yielded to the most triumphant delight. Boabdil at once resumed all the energy for which, though but by fits and starts, his earlier youth had been remarkable.

"Allah Achbar! God is great!" cried he; "we will not remain here till it suit the foe to confine the eagle again to his eyry. They have left us, — we will burst on them. Summon our *alfaquis;* we will proclaim a holy war! The sovereign of the last possessions of the Moors is in the field. Not a town that contains a Moslem but shall receive our summons, and we will gather round our standard all the children of our faith!"

"May the king live forever!" cried the council, with one voice.

"Lose not a moment," resumed Boabdil; "on to the Vivarrambla, marshal the troops, — Muza heads the cavalry, myself our foot. Ere the sun's shadow reach yonder forest, our army shall be on its march."

The warriors, hastily and in joy, left the palace; and when he was alone, Boabdil again relapsed into his wonted irresolution. After striding to and fro for some minutes in anxious thought, he abruptly quitted the hall of council, and passed into the more private chambers of the palace, till he came to a door strongly guarded by plates of iron. It yielded easily, however, to a small key which he carried in his girdle, and Boabdil stood in a small circular room, apparently without other door or outlet; but after looking cautiously round, the king touched a secret spring in the wall, which, giving way, discovered a niche, in which stood a small lamp burning with the purest naphtha, and a scroll of yellow parchment covered with strange letters and hieroglyphics. He thrust the scroll in his bosom, took the lamp in his hand, and pressing another spring within the niche, the wall receded, and showed a narrow and winding staircase. The king reclosed the entrance and descended; the stairs led at last into damp and rough passages, and the murmur of waters, that reached his ear through the thick walls, indicated the subterranean nature of the soil through which they were hewn. The lamp burned clear and steady through the darkness of the place, and Boabdil proceeded with such impatient rapidity that the distance (in reality considerable) which he traversed before he arrived at his destined bourn was quickly measured. He came at last into a wide cavern, guarded by doors concealed and secret as those which had screened the entrance from the upper air. He was in one of the many vaults which made the mighty cemetery of the monarchs of Granada; and before him stood the robed and crowned skeleton, and before him glowed the magic dial-plate of which he had spoken in his interview with Muza.

"O dread and awful image!" cried the king, throwing himself on his knees before the skeleton, — "shadow of what was once a king wise in council and terrible in war, if in those hollow bones yet lurks the impalpable and unseen spirit, hear thy repentant son. Forgive, while it is yet time, the rebellion of his fiery youth, and suffer thy daring soul to animate the doubt and weakness of his own. I go forth to battle, waiting not the signal thou didst ordain. Let not the penance for a rashness to which fate urges me on attach to my country, but to me. And if I perish in the field, may my evil destinies be buried with me, and a worthier monarch redeem my errors and preserve Granada!"

As the king raised his looks, the ᵗ unrelaxed grin of the grim dead, made yet more hideous by the mockery of the diadem and the royal robe, froze back to ice the passion and sorrow at his heart. He shuddered, and rose with a deep

sigh; when, as his eyes mechanically followed the lifted arm
of the skeleton, he beheld, with mingled delight and awe, the
hitherto motionless finger of the dial-plate pass slowly on,
and rest at the word so long and so impatiently desired.
"ARM!" cried the king; "do I read aright, — are my
prayers heard?" A low and deep sound, like that of sub-.
terranean thunder, boomed through the chamber; and in the
same instant the wall opened, and the king beheld the long-
expected figure of Almamen the magician. But no longer
was that stately form clad in the loose and peaceful garb of
the Eastern santon. Complete armour cased his broad chest
and sinewy limbs; his head alone was bare, and his prominent and impressive features were lighted, not with mystical
enthusiasm, but with warlike energy. In his right hand he
carried a drawn sword; his left supported the staff of a snow-
white and dazzling banner.

So sudden was the apparition, and so excited the mind of
the king, that the sight of a supernatural being could scarcely
have impressed him with more amaze and awe.

"King of Granada," said Almamen, "the hour hath come
at last; go forth and conquer! With the Christian monarch
there is no hope of peace or compact. At thy request I
sought him, but my spells alone preserved the life of thy
herald. Rejoice! for thine evil destinies have rolled away
from thy spirit, like a cloud from the glory of the sun. The
genii of the East have woven this banner from the rays of
benignant stars. It shall beam before thee in the front of
battle, — it shall rise over the rivers of Christian blood. As
the moon sways the bosom of the tides, it shall sway and
direct the surges and the course of war!"

"Man of mystery, thou hast given me a new life!"

"And, fighting by thy side," resumed Almamen, "I will
assist to carve out for thee, from the ruins of Arragon and
Castile, the grandeur of a new throne. Arm, monarch of
Granada, arm! I hear the neigh of thy charger in the midst
of the mailed thousands. Arm!"

BOOK IV.

CHAPTER I.

LEILA IN THE CASTLE. — THE SIEGE.

THE calmer contemplations and more holy anxieties of
Leila were at length broken in upon by intelligence, the
fearful interest of which absorbed the whole mind and care
of every inhabitant of the castle. Boabdil el Chico had taken
the field, at the head of a numerous army. Rapidly scouring
the country, he had descended, one after one, upon the principal fortresses, which Ferdinand had left, strongly garrisoned,
in the immediate neighbourhood. His success was as immediate as it was signal; the terror of his arms began once more
to spread far and wide; every day swelled his ranks with new
recruits; and from the snow-clad summits of the Sierra
Nevada poured down, in wild hordes, the fierce mountain
race, who, accustomed to eternal winter, made a strange contrast, in their rugged appearance and shaggy clothing, to the
glittering and civilized soldiery of Granada.

Moorish towns, which had submitted to Ferdinand, broke
from their allegiance, and sent their ardent youth and experienced veterans to the standard of the Keys and Crescent. To
add to the sudden panic of the Spaniards, it went forth that a
formidable magician, who seemed inspired rather with the
fury of a demon than the valour of a man, had made an
abrupt appearance in the ranks of the Moslems. Wherever
the Moors shrank back from wall or tower, down which
poured the boiling pitch, or rolled the deadly artillery of the
besieged, this sorcerer — rushing into the midst of the flag-
ging force, and waving, with wild gestures, a white banner,
supposed by both Moor and Christian to be the work of magic
and preternatural spells — dared every danger and escaped

every weapon; with voice, with prayer, with example, he fired the Moors to an enthusiasm that revived the first days of Mohammedan conquest; and tower after tower, along the mighty range of the mountain-chain of fortresses, was polluted by the wave and glitter of the ever-victorious banner. The veteran Mendo de Quexada, who with a garrison of two hundred and fifty men held the castle of Alhendin, was, however, undaunted by the unprecedented successes of Boabdil. Aware of the approaching storm, he spent the days of peace yet accorded to him in making every preparation for the siege that he foresaw: messengers were despatched to Ferdinand; new outworks were added to the castle; ample store of provisions was laid in; and no precaution omitted that could still preserve to the Spaniards a fortress that, from its vicinity to Granada, its command of the Vega and the valleys of the Alpuxarras, was the bitterest thorn in the side of the Moorish power.

It was early one morning that Leila stood by the lattice of her lofty chamber, gazing, with many and mingled emotions, on the distant domes of Granada as they slept in the silent sunshine. Her heart for the moment was busy with the thoughts of home, and the chances and peril of the time were forgotten.

The sound of martial music afar off broke upon her reveries; she started, and listened breathlessly: it became more distinct and clear. The clash of the zell, the boom of the African drum, and the wild and barbarous blast of the Moorish clarion were now each distinguishable from the other; and at length, as she gazed and listened, winding along the steeps of the mountain were seen the gleaming spears and pennants of the Moslem vanguard. Another moment, and the whole castle was astir.

Mendo de Quexada, hastily arming, repaired, himself, to the battlements, and from her lattice Leila beheld him, from time to time, stationing to the best advantage his scanty troops. In a few minutes she was joined by Donna Inez and the women of the castle, who fearfully clustered round their mistress, — not the less disposed, however, to gratify the passion of the sex by a glimpse through the lattice at the gorgeous array of the Moorish army.

The casements of Leila's chamber were peculiarly adapted to command a safe nor insufficient view of the progress of the enemy; and with a beating heart and flushing cheek the Jewish maiden, deaf to the voices around her, imagined she could already descry amidst the horsemen the lion port and snowy garments of Muza Ben Abil Gazan.

What a situation was hers! Already a Christian, could she hope for the success of the infidel? Ever a woman, could she hope for the defeat of her lover? But the time for meditation on her destiny was but brief; the detachment of the Moorish cavalry was now just without the walls of the little town that girded the castle, and the loud clarion of the heralds summoned the garrison to surrender.

"Not while one stone stands upon another!" was the short answer of Quexada; and in ten minutes afterwards the sullen roar of the artillery broke from wall and tower over the vales below.

It was then that the women, from Leila's lattice, beheld, slowly marshalling themselves in order, the whole power and pageantry of the besieging army. Thick, serried, — line after line, column upon column, — they spread below the frowning steep. The sunbeams lighted up that goodly array as it swayed and murmured and advanced, like the billows of a glittering sea. The royal standard was soon descried waving above the pavilion of Boabdil; and the king himself, mounted on his cream-coloured charger, which was covered with trappings of cloth-of-gold, was recognized amongst the infantry, whose task it was to lead the assault.

"Pray with us, my daughter!" cried Inez, falling on her knees. Alas! what could Leila pray for?

Four days and four nights passed away in that memorable siege; for the moon, then at her full, allowed no respite even in night itself. Their numbers and their vicinity to Granada gave the besiegers the advantage of constant relays, and troop succeeded to troop, so that the weary had ever successors in the vigour of new assailants.

On the fifth day all of the fortress, save the keep (an immense tower), was in the hands of the Moslems; and in this last hold, the worn-out and scanty remnant of the garrison mustered, in the last hope of a brave despair.

Quexada appeared, covered with gore and dust, — his eyes bloodshot, his cheek haggard and hollow, his locks blanched with sudden age, — in the hall of the tower where the women, half dead with terror, were assembled.

"Food!" cried he, — "food and wine! It may be our last banquet."

His wife threw her arms round him. "Not yet," he cried, "not yet; we will have one embrace before we part."

"Is there, then, no hope?" said Inez, with a pale cheek, yet steady eye.

"None, unless to-morrow's dawn gild the spears of Ferdinand's army upon yonder hills. Till morn we may hold out." As he spoke, he hastily devoured some morsels of food, drained a huge goblet of wine, and abruptly quitted the chamber.

At that moment the women distinctly heard the loud shouts of the Moors; and Leila, approaching the grated casement, could perceive the approach of what seemed to her like moving walls.

Covered by ingenious constructions of wood and thick hides, the besiegers advanced to the foot of the tower in comparative shelter from the burning streams which still poured, fast and seething, from the battlements; while in the rear came showers of darts and cross-bolts from the more distant Moors, protecting the work of the engineer, and piercing through almost every loophole and crevice in the fortress.

Meanwhile the stalwart governor beheld with dismay and despair the preparations of the engineers, whom the wooden screen-works protected from every weapon.

"By the Holy Sepulchre," cried he, gnashing his teeth, "they are mining the tower, and we shall be buried in its ruins! Look out, Gonsalvo; see you not a gleam of spears yonder, over the mountain? Mine eyes are dim with watching."

"Alas! brave Mendo, it is only the sloping sun upon the snows; but there is hope yet."

The soldier's words terminated in a shrill and sudden cry of agony; and he fell dead by the side of Quexada, the brain crushed by a bolt from a Moorish arquebus.

"My best warrior!" said Quexada; "peace be with him! Ho, there! See you yon desperate infidel urging on the miners? By the heavens above, it is he of the white banner; it is the sorcerer! Fire on him! he is without the shelter of the woodworks."

Twenty shafts, from wearied and nerveless arms, fell innocuous round the form of Almamen; and as, waving aloft his ominous banner, he disappeared again behind the screenworks, the Spaniards almost fancied they could hear his exulting and demon laugh.

The sixth day came, and the work of the enemy was completed. The tower was entirely undermined; the foundations rested only upon wooden props, which, with a humanity that was characteristic of Boabdil, had been placed there, in order that the besieged might escape ere the final crash of their last hold.

It was now noon; the whole Moorish force, quitting the plain, occupied the steep that spread below the tower, in multitudinous array and breathless expectation. The miners stood aloof; the Spaniards lay prostrate and exhausted upon the battlements, like mariners who, after every effort against the storm, await, resigned and almost indifferent, the sweep of the fatal surge.

Suddenly the lines of the Moors gave way, and Boabdil himself, with Muza at his right hand, and Almamen on his left, advanced towards the foot of the tower. At the same time the Ethiopian guards, each bearing a torch, marched slowly in the rear, and from the midst of them paced the royal herald and sounded the last warning. The hush of the immense armament; the glare of the torches, lighting the ebon faces and giant forms of their bearers; the majestic appearance of the king himself; the heroic aspect of Muza; the bare head and glittering banner of Almamen, — all combined with the circumstances of the time to invest the spectacle with something singularly awful, and perhaps sublime.

Quexada turned his eyes mutely round the ghastly faces of his warriors, and still made not the signal. His lips muttered, his eyes glared, when suddenly he heard below the wail of women; and the thought of Inez, the bride of his youth, the partner of his age, came upon him, and with a trembling hand he lowered the yet unquailing standard of Spain. Then the silence below broke into a mighty shout, which shook the grim tower to its unsteady and temporary base.

"Arise, my friends," he said, with a bitter sigh; "we have fought like men, and our country will not blush for us."

He descended the winding stairs; his soldiers followed him with faltering steps; the gates of the keep unfolded; and these gallant Christians surrendered themselves to the Moor.

"Do with *us* as you will," said Quexada, as he laid the keys at the hoofs of Boabdil's barb; "but there are women in the garrison, who —"

"Are sacred," interrupted the king. "At once we accord their liberty, and free transport whithersoever ye would desire. Speak, then: to what place of safety shall they be conducted?"

"Generous king!" replied the veteran Quexada, brushing away his tears with the back of his hand, "you take the sting from our shame. We accept your offer in the same spirit in which it is made. Across the mountains, on the verge of the plain of Olfadez, I possess a small castle, ungarrisoned and unfortified. Thence, should the war take that direction, the women can readily obtain safe-conduct to the queen at Cordova."

"Be it so," returned Boabdil. Then, with Oriental delicacy, selecting the eldest of the officers round him, he gave him instructions to enter the castle, and with a strong guard provide for the safety of the women, according to the directions of Quexada. To another of his officers he confided the Spanish prisoners, and gave the signal to his army to withdraw from the spot, leaving only a small body to complete the ruin of the fortress.

Accompanied by Almamen and his principal officers, Boabdil now hastened towards Granada; and while, with slower progress, Quexada and his companions, under a strong escort, took their way across the Vega, a sudden turn in their course brought abruptly before them the tower they had so valiantly defended. There it still stood, proud and stern, amidst the blackened and broken wrecks around it, shooting aloft, dark and grim, against the sky. Another moment, and a mighty crash sounded on their ears, while the tower fell to the earth amidst volumes of wreathing smoke and showers of dust, which were borne by the concussion to the spot on which they took their last gaze of the proudest fortress on which the Moors of Granada had beheld, from their own walls, the standard of Arragon and Castile.

At the same time Leila, — thus brought so strangely within the very reach of her father and her lover, and yet by a mysterious fate still divided from both, — with Donna Inez and the rest of the females of the garrison, pursued her melancholy path along the ridges of the mountains.

CHAPTER II.

ALMAMEN'S PROPOSED ENTERPRISE. — THE THREE ISRAELITES. — CIRCUMSTANCE IMPRESSES EACH CHARACTER WITH A VARYING DIE.

BOABDIL followed up his late success with a series of brilliant assaults on the neighbouring fortresses. Granada, like a strong man bowed to the ground, wrenched, one after one, the bands that had crippled her liberty and strength; and at length, after regaining a considerable portion of the surrounding territory, the king resolved to lay siege to the sea-port of Salobreña. Could he obtain this town, Boabdil, by establishing communication between the sea and Granada, would both be enabled to avail himself of the assistance of his African allies, and also prevent the Spaniards from cutting off supplies to the city, should they again besiege it. Thither, then, accompanied by Muza, the Moorish king bore his victorious standard.

On the eve of his departure Almamen sought the king's presence. A great change had come over the santon since the departure of Ferdinand, — his wonted stateliness of mien was gone; his eyes were sunk and hollow; his manner, disturbed and absent. In fact, his love for his daughter made the sole softness of his character; and that daughter was in the hands of the king who had sentenced the father to the tortures of the Inquisition! To what dangers might she not be subjected by the intolerant zeal of conversion! And could that frame and gentle heart brave the terrific engines that might be brought against her fears? "Better," thought he, "that she should perish, even by the torture, than adopt that hated faith." He gnashed his teeth in agony at either alternative. His dreams, his objects, his revenge, his ambition,—all forsook him; one single hope, one thought, completely mastered his stormy passions and fitful intellect.

In this mood the pretended santon met Boabdil. He represented to the king, over whom his influence had prodigiously increased since the late victories of the Moors, the necessity of employing the armies of Ferdinand at a distance. He proposed, in furtherance of this policy, to venture himself in Cordova, to endeavour secretly to stir up those Moors in that, their ancient kingdom, who had succumbed to the Spanish yoke, and whose hopes might naturally be inflamed by the recent successes of Boabdil, and at least to foment such disturbances as might afford the king sufficient time to complete his designs and recruit his force by aid of the powers with which he was in league.

The representations of Almamen at length conquered Boabdil's reluctance to part with his sacred guide, and it was finally arranged that the Israelite should at once depart from the city.

As Almamen pursued homeward his solitary way, he found himself suddenly accosted in the Hebrew tongue. He turned hastily, and saw before him an old man in the Jewish gown.

He recognized Elias, one of the wealthiest and most eminent of the race of Israel.

"Pardon me, wise countryman," said the Jew, bowing to the earth, "but I cannot resist the temptation of claiming kindred with one through whom the horn of Israel may be so triumphantly exalted."

"Hush, man!" said Almamen, quickly, and looking sharply round; "I thy countryman! Art thou not, as thy speech betokens, an Israelite?"

"Yea," returned the Jew, "and of the same tribe as thy honoured father, peace be with his ashes! I remembered thee at once, boy though thou wert when thy steps shook off the dust against Granada. I remembered thee, I say, at once, on thy return; but I have kept thy secret, trusting that, through thy soul and genius, thy fallen brethren might put off sackcloth and feast upon the house-tops."

Almamen looked hard at the keen, sharp Arab features of the Jew; and at length he answered, "And how can Israel be restored? Wilt thou fight for her?"

"I am too old, son of Issachar, to bear arms; but our tribes are many, and our youth strong. Amid these disturbances between dog and dog — "

"The lion may get his own," interrupted Almamen, impetuously; "let us hope it. Hast thou heard of the new persecutions against us that the false Nazarene king has already commenced in Cordova, — persecutions that make the heart sick and the blood cold?"

"Alas!" replied Elias, "such woes indeed have not failed to reach mine ear; and I have kindred, near and beloved kindred, wealthy and honoured men, scattered throughout that land."

"Were it not better that they should die on the field than by the rack?" exclaimed Almamen, fiercely. "God of my fathers! if there be yet a spark of manhood left amongst thy people, let thy servant fan it to a flame that shall burn as the fire burns the stubble, so that the earth may bare before the blaze!"

"Nay," said Elias, dismayed rather than excited by the vehemence of his comrade, "be not rash, son of Issachar, be not rash; peradventure thou wilt but exasperate the wrath of the rulers, and our substance thereby will be utterly consumed."

Almamen drew back, placed his hand quietly on the Jew's shoulder, looked him hard in the face, and, gently laughing, turned away.

Elias did not attempt to arrest his steps. "Impracticable," he muttered; "impracticable and dangerous! I always thought so. He may do us harm: were he not so strong and fierce, I would put my knife under his left rib. Verily, gold is a great thing; and— Out on me! the knaves at home will be wasting the oil, now they know old Elias is abroad." Thereat the Jew drew his cloak around him, and quickened his pace.

Almamen in the mean while sought, through dark and subterranean passages known only to himself, his accustomed home. He passed much of the night alone; but ere the morning star announced to the mountain-tops the presence of the sun, he stood, prepared for his journey, in his secret vault, by the door of the subterranean passages, with old Ximen beside him.

"I go, Ximen," said Almamen, "upon a doubtful quest. Whether I discover my daughter and succeed in bearing her in safety from their contaminating grasp, or whether I fall into their snares and perish, there is an equal chance that I may return no more to Granada. Should this be so, you will be heir to such wealth as I leave in these places: I know that your age will be consoled for the lack of children when your eyes look upon the laugh of gold."

Ximen bowed low, and mumbled out some inaudible protestations and thanks. Almamen sighed heavily as he looked round the room. "I have evil omens in my soul, and evil prophecies in my books," said he, mournfully; "but the worst is here," he added, putting his finger significantly to his temples. "The string is stretched; one more blow would snap it."

As he thus said, he opened the door and vanished through that labyrinth of galleries by which he was enabled at all times to reach unobserved either the palace of the Alhambra or the gardens without the gates of the city.

Ximen remained behind a few moments in deep thought. "All mine if he dies," said he; "all mine if he does not return! All mine, all mine! and I have not a child nor a kinsman in the world to clutch it away from me!" With that he locked the vault, and returned to the upper air.

CHAPTER III.

THE FUGITIVE AND THE MEETING.

In their different directions the rival kings were equally successful. Salobreña, but lately conquered by the Christians, was thrown into a commotion by the first glimpse of Boabdil's banners; the populace rose, beat back their Christian guards, and opened the gates to the last of their race of kings. The garrison alone, to which the Spaniards retreated, resisted Boabdil's arms, and, defended by impregnable walls, promised an obstinate and bloody siege.

Meanwhile, Ferdinand had no sooner entered Cordova than his extensive scheme of confiscation and holy persecution commenced. Not only did more than five hundred Jews perish in the dark and secret gripe of the Grand Inquisitor, but several hundred of the wealthiest Christian families, in whose blood was detected the hereditary Jewish taint, were thrown into prison; and such as were most fortunate purchased life by the sacrifice of half their treasures. At this time, however, there suddenly broke forth a formidable insurrection amongst those miserable subjects, — the Messenians of the Iberian Sparta. The Jews were so far aroused from their long debasement by omnipotent despair that a single spark, falling on the ashes of their ancient spirit, rekindled the flame of the descendants of the fierce warriors of Palestine. They were encouraged and assisted by the suspected Christians who had been involved in the same persecution; and the whole was headed by a man who appeared suddenly amongst them, and whose fiery eloquence and martial spirit produced, at such a season, the most fervent enthusiasm. Unhappily, the whole details of this singular outbreak are withheld from us; only by wary hints and guarded allusions do the Spanish chroniclers apprise us of its existence and its perils. It is clear that all narrative of an event that might afford the most dangerous precedent, and was alarming to the pride and avarice of the Spanish king, as well as the pious zeal of the Church, was strictly forbidden; and the conspiracy was hushed in the dread silence of the Inquisition, into whose hands the principal conspirators ultimately fell. We learn only that a determined and sanguinary struggle was followed by the triumph of Ferdinand and the complete extinction of the treason.

It was one evening that a solitary fugitive, hard chased by an armed troop of the brothers of St. Hermandad, was seen emerging from a wild and rocky defile which opened abruptly on the gardens of a small and, by the absence of fortification and sentries, seemingly deserted castle. Behind him, in the exceeding stillness which characterizes the air of a Spanish twilight, he heard, at a considerable distance, the blast of the horn and the tramp of hoofs. His pursuers, divided into several detachments, were scouring the country after him, as the fishermen draw their nets from bank to bank, conscious that the prey they drive before the meshes cannot escape them at the last. The fugitive halted in doubt, and gazed round him. He was wellnigh exhausted; his eyes were blood-shot; the large drops rolled fast down his brow; his whole frame quivered and palpitated like that of a stag when he stands at bay. Beyond the castle spread a broad plain far as the eye could reach, without shrub or hollow to conceal his form; flight across a space so favourable to his pursuers was evidently in vain. No alternative was left, unless he turned back on the very path taken by the horsemen, or trusted to such scanty and perilous shelter as the copses in the castle garden might afford him. He decided on the latter refuge, cleared the low and lonely wall that girded the demesne, and plunged into a thicket of overhanging oaks and chestnuts.

At that hour and in that garden, by the side of a little

fountain, were seated two females, — the one of mature and somewhat advanced years; the other in the flower of virgin youth. But the flower was prematurely faded; and neither the bloom, nor sparkle, nor undulating play of feature that should have suited her age was visible in the marble paleness and contemplative sadness of her beautiful countenance.

"Alas! my young friend," said the elder of these ladies, "it is in these hours of solitude and calm that we are most deeply impressed with the nothingness of life. Thou, my sweet convert, art now the object, no longer of my compassion, but my envy; and earnestly do I feel convinced of the blessed repose thy spirit will enjoy in the lap of the Mother Church. Happy are they who die young, but thrice happy they who die in the spirit rather than the flesh, — dead to sin, but not to virtue; to terror, not to hope; to man, but not to God!"

"Dear Señora," replied the young maiden, mournfully, "were I alone on earth, Heaven is my witness with what deep and thankful resignation I should take the holy vows and forswear the past; but the heart remains human, however divine the hope that it may cherish. And sometimes I start, and think of home, of childhood, of my strange but beloved father, deserted and childless in his old age."

"Thine, Leila," returned the elder señora, "are but the sorrows our nature is doomed to. What matter, whether absence or death sever the affections? Thou lamentest a father; I, a son dead in the pride of his youth and beauty, — a husband languishing in the fetters of the Moor. Take comfort for thy sorrows in the reflection that sorrow is the heritage of all."

Ere Leila could reply, the orange-boughs that sheltered the spot where they sat were put aside, and between the women and the fountain stood the dark form of Almamen the Israelite. Leila rose, shrieked, and flung herself, unconscious, on his breast.

"O Lord of Israel!" cried Almamen, in a tone of deep anguish, "do I then at last regain my child? Do I press her to my heart? And is it only for that brief moment, when I stand upon the brink of death? Leila, my child, look up, —

smile upon thy father; let him feel, on his maddening and burning brow, the sweet breath of the last of his race, and bear with him at least one holy and gentle thought to the dark grave."

"My father, is it indeed my father?" said Leila, recovering herself, and drawing back, that she might assure herself of that familiar face. "It is thou! it is, it is! Oh, what blessed chance brings us together?"

"That chance is the destiny that hurries me to my tomb," answered Almamen, solemnly. "Hark! hear you not the sound of their rushing steeds, their impatient voices? They are on me now!"

"Who? Of whom speakest thou?"

"My pursuers, — the horsemen of the Spaniard."

"Oh, Señora, save him!" cried Leila, turning to Donna Inez, whom both father and child had hitherto forgotten, and who now stood gazing upon Almamen with wondering and anxious eyes. "Whither can he fly? The vaults of the castle may conceal him. This way; hasten!"

"Stay," said Inez, trembling, and approaching close to Almamen. "Do I see aright, and amidst the dark change of years and trial do I recognize that stately form which once contrasted to the sad eye of a mother the drooping and faded form of her only son? Art thou not he who saved my boy from the pestilence, who accompanied him to the shores of Naples, and consigned him to these arms? Look on me! Dost thou not recall the mother of thy friend?"

"I recall thy features dimly and as in a dream," answered the Hebrew; "and while thou speakest, there rush upon me the memories of an earlier time, in lands where Leila first looked upon the day, and her mother sang to me at sunset by the stream of the Euphrates and on the sites of departed empires. Thy son — I remember now; I had friendship then with a Christian, for I was still young."

"Waste not the time, Father, Señora!" cried Leila, impatiently, clinging still to her father's breast.

"You are right; nor shall your sire, in whom I thus wonderfully recognize my son's friend, perish if I can save him."

Inez then conducted her strange guest to a small door in the rear of the castle; and after leading him through some of the principal apartments, left him in one of the tiring-rooms adjoining her own chamber, and the entrance to which the arras concealed. She rightly judged this a safer retreat than the vaults of the castle might afford, since her great name and known intimacy with Isabel would preclude all suspicion of her abetting in the escape of the fugitive, and keep those places the most secure in which, without such aid, he could not have secreted himself.

In a few minutes several of the troop arrived at the castle; and on learning the name of its owner, contented themselves with searching the gardens and the lower and more exposed apartments, and then, recommending to the servants a vigilant look-out, remounted, and proceeded to scour the plain, over which now slowly fell the starlight and shade of night. When Leila stole at last to the room in which Almamen was hid, she found him, stretched on his mantle, in a deep sleep. Exhausted by all he had undergone, and his rigid nerves, as it were, relaxed by the sudden softness of that interview with his child, the slumber of that fiery wanderer was as calm as an infant's; and their relation almost seemed reversed, and the daughter to be as a mother watching over her offspring, when Leila seated herself softly by him, fixing her eyes — to which the tears came ever, ever to be brushed away — upon his worn but tranquil features, made yet more serene by the quiet light that glimmered through the casement. And so passed the hours of that night; and the father and the child — the meek convert, the revengeful fanatic — were under the same roof.

CHAPTER IV.

ALMAMEN HEARS AND SEES, BUT REFUSES TO BELIEVE; FOR
THE BRAIN, OVERWROUGHT, GROWS DULL, EVEN IN THE
KEENEST.

THE dawn broke slowly upon the chamber, and Almamen
still slept. It was the Sabbath of the Christians, — that day
on which the Saviour rose from the dead; thence named so
emphatically and sublimely by the Early Church THE LORD'S
DAY.[1] And as the ray of the sun flashed in the east, it fell
like a glory over a crucifix placed in the deep recess of the
Gothic casement, and brought startlingly before the eyes of
Leila that face upon which the rudest of the Catholic sculp-
tors rarely fail to preserve the mystic and awful union of the
expiring anguish of the man with the lofty patience of the
God. It looked upon her, that face; it invited, it encouraged, while it thrilled and subdued. She stole gently from
the side of her father; she crept to the spot, and flung herself
on her knees beside the consecrated image.

"Support me, O Redeemer!" she murmured; "support thy
creature! strengthen her steps in the blessed path, though it
divide her irrevocably from all that on earth she loves. And
if there be a sacrifice in her solemn choice, accept, O Thou,
the Crucified! accept it, in part atonement of the crime of her
stubborn race; and hereafter let the lips of a maiden of
Judæa implore thee, not in vain, for some mitigation of the
awful curse that hath fallen justly upon her tribe."

As, broken by low sobs, and in a choked and muttered voice,
Leila poured forth her prayer, she was startled by a deep
groan; and turning in alarm she saw that Almamen had
awaked, and, leaning on his arm, was now bending upon her
his dark eyes, once more gleaming with all their wonted fire.

[1] Before the Christian era the Sunday was, however, called the Lord's
day, — that is, the day of the Lord the Sun.

"Speak," he said, as she coweringly hid her face, — "speak to me, or I shall be turned to stone by one horrid thought. It is not before that symbol that thou kneelest in adoration; and my sense wanders if it tell me that thy broken words expressed the worship of an apostate? In mercy, speak!"

"Father!" began Leila; but her lips refused to utter more than that touching and holy word.

Almamen rose, and plucking the hands from her face, gazed on her some moments, as if he would penetrate her very soul; and Leila, recovering her courage in the pause, by degrees met his eyes unquailing, — her pure and ingenuous brow raised to his, and sadness, but not guilt, speaking from every line of that lovely face.

"Thou dost not tremble," said Almamen, at length breaking the silence, "and I have erred. Thou art not the criminal I deemed thee. Come to my arms!"

"Alas!" said Leila, obeying the instinct, and casting herself upon that rugged bosom, "I will dare, at least, not to disavow my God. Father, by that dread anathema which is on our race, which has made us homeless and powerless, outcasts and strangers in the land, — by the persecution and anguish we have known, teach thy lordly heart that we are rightly punished for the persecution and the anguish we doomed to Him whose footstep hallowed our native earth! FIRST, IN THE HISTORY OF THE WORLD, DID THE STERN HEBREWS INFLICT UPON MANKIND THE AWFUL CRIME OF PERSECUTION FOR OPINION'S SAKE. The seed we sowed hath brought forth the Dead Sea fruit upon which we feed. I asked for resignation and for hope: I looked upon yonder cross, and I found both. Harden not thy heart; listen to thy child; wise though thou be, and weak though her woman spirit, listen to me."

"Be dumb," cried Almamen, in such a voice as might have come from the charnel, so ghostly and deathly sounded its hollow tone; then, recoiling some steps, he placed both his hands upon his temples; and muttered, "Mad, mad! yes, yes; this is but a delirium, and I am tempted with a devil!

Oh, my child," he resumed, in a voice that became, on the sudden, inexpressibly tender and imploring, "I have been sorely tried, and I dreamed a feverish dream of passion and revenge. Be thine the lips and thine the soothing hand that shall wake me from it. Let us fly forever from these hated lands; let us leave to these miserable infidels their bloody contest, careless which shall fall. To a soil on which the iron heel does not clang, to an air where man's orisons rise in solitude to the Great Jehovah, let us hasten our weary steps. Come! while the castle yet sleeps, let us forth unseen, — the father and the child. We will hold sweet commune by the way. And hark ye, Leila," he added, in a low and abrupt whisper, "talk not to me of yonder symbol; for thy God is a jealous God, and hath no likeness in the graven image."

Had he been less exhausted by long travail and racking thoughts, far different, perhaps, would have been the language of a man so stern. But circumstance impresses the hardest substance; and despite his native intellect and affected superiority over others, no one, perhaps, was more human, in his fitful moods, — his weakness and his strength, his passion and his purpose, — than that strange man who had dared, in his dark studies and arrogant self-will, to aspire beyond humanity.

That was, indeed, a perilous moment for the young convert. The unexpected softness of her father utterly subdued her; nor was she sufficiently possessed of that all-denying zeal of the Catholic enthusiast to which every human tie and earthly duty has been often sacrificed on the shrine of a rapt and metaphysical piety. Whatever her opinions, her new creed, her secret desire of the cloister, fed as it was by the sublime, though fallacious, notion that in her conversion, her sacrifice, the crimes of her race might be expiated in the eyes of Him whose death had been the great atonement of a world, — whatever such higher thoughts and sentiments, they gave way at that moment to the irresistible impulse of household nature and of filial duty. Should she desert her father, and could that desertion be a virtue? Her heart put and answered both questions in a breath. She approached Almamen, placed her hand in his, and said, steadily and calmly, "Father, wheresoever thou goest, I will wend with thee."

But Heaven ordained to each another destiny than might have been theirs, had the dictates of that impulse been fulfilled.

Ere Almamen could reply, a trumpet sounded clear and loud at the gate.

"Hark!" he said, griping his dagger, and starting back to a sense of the dangers round him. "They come, — my pursuers and my murderers; but these limbs are sacred from the rack."

Even that sound of ominous danger was almost a relief to Leila. "I will go," she said, "and learn what the blast betokens. Remain here, be cautious; I will return."

Several minutes, however, elapsed before Leila reappeared; she was accompanied by Donna Inez, whose paleness and agitation betokened her alarm. A courier had arrived at the gate to announce the approach of the queen, who with a considerable force was on her way to join Ferdinand, then, in the usual rapidity of his movements, before one of the Moorish towns that had revolted from his allegiance. It was impossible for Almamen to remain in safety in the castle, and the only hope of escape was departing immediately and in disguise.

"I have," she said, "a trusty and faithful servant with me in the castle, to whom I can, without anxiety, confide the charge of your safety; and even if suspected by the way, my name, and the companionship of my servant, will remove all obstacles. It is not a long journey hence to Guadix, which has already revolted to the Moors; there, till the armies of Ferdinand surround the walls, your refuge may be secure."

Almamen remained for some moments plunged in a gloomy silence; but at length he signified his assent to the plan proposed, and Donna Inez hastened to give the directions to his intended guide.

"Leila," said the Hebrew, when left alone with his daughter, "think not that it is for mine own safety that I stoop to

8

this flight from thee. No. But never till thou wert lost to me, by mine own rash confidence in another, did I know how dear to my heart was the last scion of my race, the sole memorial left to me of thy mother's love. Regaining thee once more, a new and a soft existence opens upon my eyes, and the earth seems to change, as by a sudden revolution, from winter into spring. For thy sake I consent to use all the means that man's intellect can devise for preservation from my foes. Meanwhile, here will rest my soul; to this spot, within one week from this period, — no matter through what danger I pass, — I shall return; then I shall claim thy promise. I will arrange all things for our flight, and no stone shall harm thy footstep by the way. The Lord of Israel be with thee, my daughter, and strengthen thy heart! But," he added, tearing himself from her embrace, as he heard steps ascending to the chamber, "deem not that, in this most fond and fatherly affection, I forget what is due to me and thee. Think not that my love is only the brute and insensate feeling of the progenitor to the offspring: I love thee for thy mother's sake; I love thee for thine own; I love thee yet more for the sake of Israel. If thou perish, if thou art lost to us, thou, the last daughter of the house of Issachar, then the haughtiest family of God's great people is extinct."

Here Inez appeared at the door, but withdrew, at the impatient and lordly gesture of Almamen, who, without further heed of the interruption, resumed, —

"I look to thee and thy seed for the regeneration which I once trusted, fool that I was, mine own day might see effected. Let this pass. Thou art under the roof of the Nazarene. I will not believe that the arts we have resisted against fire and sword can prevail with thee. But if I err, awful will be the penalty! Could I once know that thou hadst forsaken thy ancestral creed, though warrior and priest stood by thee, though thousands and ten thousands were by thy right hand, this steel should save the race of Issachar from dishonour. Beware! Thou weepest; but, child, I warn, not threaten. God be with thee!"

He wrung the cold hand of his child, turned to the door,

and after such disguise as the brief time allowed him could afford, quitted the castle with his Spanish guide, who, accustomed to the benevolence of his mistress, obeyed her injunction without wonder, though not without suspicion.

The third part of an hour had scarcely elapsed, and the sun was yet on the mountain-tops, when Isabel arrived.

She came to announce that the outbreaks of the Moorish towns in the vicinity rendered the half-fortified castle of her friend no longer a secure abode; and she honoured the Spanish lady with a command to accompany her, with her female suite, to the camp of Ferdinand.

Leila received the intelligence with a kind of stupor. Her interview with her father, the strong and fearful contests of emotion which that interview occasioned, left her senses faint and dizzy; and when she found herself, by the twilight star, once more with the train of Isabel, the only feeling that stirred actively through her stunned and bewildered mind was that the hand of Providence conducted her from a temptation that, the Reader of all hearts knew, the daughter and woman would have been too feeble to resist.

On the fifth day from his departure Almamen returned, — to find the castle deserted, and his daughter gone.

CHAPTER V.

IN THE FERMENT OF GREAT EVENTS THE DREGS RISE.

THE Israelites did not limit their struggles to the dark conspiracy to which allusion has been made. In some of the Moorish towns that revolted from Ferdinand, they renounced the neutrality they had hitherto maintained between Christian and Moslem. Whether it was that they were inflamed by the fearful and wholesale barbarities enforced by Ferdinand and the Inquisition against their tribe; or whether they were stirred up by one of their own order, in whom was recognized the head of their most sacred family; or whether, as is most probable, both causes combined, — certain it is that they manifested a feeling that was thoroughly unknown to the ordinary habits and policy of that peaceable people. They bore great treasure to the public stock, they demanded arms, and, under their own leaders, were admitted, though with much jealousy and precaution, into the troops of the arrogant and disdainful Moslems.

In this conjunction of hostile planets, Ferdinand had recourse to his favourite policy of wile and stratagem. Turning against the Jews the very treaty Almamen had once sought to obtain in their favour, he caused it to be circulated privately that the Jews, anxious to purchase their peace with him, had promised to betray the Moorish towns and Granada itself into his hands. The paper, which Ferdinand himself had signed in his interview with Almamen, and of which, on the capture of the Hebrew, he had taken care to repossess himself, he gave to a spy, whom he sent, disguised as a Jew, into one of the revolted cities.

Private intelligence reached the Moorish ringleader of the arrival of this envoy. He was seized, and the document found on his person. The form of the words drawn up by Almamen (who had carefully omitted mention of his own name, — whether that which he assumed, or that which, by birth, he should have borne) merely conveyed the compact that if by a Jew, within two weeks from the date therein specified, Granada was delivered to the Christian king, the Jews should enjoy certain immunities and rights.

The discovery of this document filled the Moors of the city to which the spy had been sent with a fury that no words can describe. Always distrusting their allies, they now imagined they perceived the sole reason of their sudden enthusiasm, of their demand for arms. The mob rose; the principal Jews were seized and massacred without trial, — some by the wrath of the multitude, some by the slower tortures of the magistrate. Messengers were sent to the different revolted towns, and, above all, to Granada itself, to put the Moslems on their guard against these unhappy enemies of either party. At once covetous and ferocious, the Moors rivalled the Inquisition in their cruelty, and Ferdinand in their extortion.

It was the dark fate of Almamen, as of most premature and heated liberators of the enslaved, to double the terrors and the evils he had sought to cure. The warning arrived at Granada at a time in which the vizier, Jusef, had received the commands of his royal master, still at the siege of Salobreña, to use every exertion to fill the wasting treasuries. Fearful of new exactions against the Moors, the vizier hailed as a message from Heaven so just a pretext for a new and sweeping impost on the Jews. The spendthrift violence of the mob was restrained, because it was headed by the authorities, who were wisely anxious that the State should have no rival in the plunder it required; and the work of confiscation and robbery was carried on with a majestic and calm regularity which redounded no less to the credit of Jusef than it contributed to the coffers of the king.

It was late one evening when Ximen was making his usual round through the chambers of Almamen's house. As he glanced around at the various articles of wealth and luxury, he ever and anon burst into a low, fitful chuckle, rubbed his lean hands, and mumbled out: "If my master should die! if my master should die!"

While thus engaged, he heard a confused and distant shout; and listening attentively, he distinguished a cry, grown of late sufficiently familiar, of "Live, Jusef the just, — perish, the traitor Jews!"

"Ah," said Ximen, as the whole character of his face changed; "some new robbery upon our race. And this is thy work, son of Issachar! Madman that thou wert, to be wiser than thy sires, and seek to dupe the idolaters in the council-chamber and the camp, — their field, their vantage-ground; as the bazaar and the market-place are ours. None suspect that the potent santon is the traitor Jew, but I know it. I could give thee to the bow-string; and if thou wert dead, all thy goods and gold, even to the mule at the manger, would be old Ximen's."

He paused at that thought, shut his eyes, and smiled at the

prospect his fancy conjured up; and completing his survey, retired to his own chamber, which opened, by a small door, upon one of the back courts. He had scarcely reached the room when he heard a low tap at the outer door, and when it was thrice repeated, he knew that it was one of his Jewish brethren; for Ximen — as years, isolation, and avarice gnawed away whatever of virtue once put forth some meagre fruit from a heart naturally bare and rocky — still preserved one human feeling towards his countrymen. It was the bond which unites all the persecuted; and Ximen loved them, because he could not envy their happiness. The power, the knowledge, the lofty, though wild, designs of his master, stung and humbled him; he secretly hated, because he could not compassionate or contemn him. But the bowed frame and slavish voice and timid nerves of his crushed brotherhood presented to the old man the likeness of things that could not exult over him. Debased and aged and solitary as he was, he felt a kind of wintry warmth in the thought that even *he* had the power to protect!

He thus maintained an intercourse with his fellow Israelites, and often in their dangers had afforded them a refuge in the numerous vaults and passages, the ruins of which may still be descried beneath the mouldering foundations of that mysterious mansion. And as the house was generally supposed the property of an absent emir, and had been especially recommended to the care of the cadis by Boabdil, who alone of the Moors knew it as one of the dwelling-places of the santon, whose ostensible residence was in apartments allotted to him within the palace, — it was perhaps the sole place within Granada which afforded an unsuspected and secure refuge to the hunted Israelites.

When Ximen recognized the wonted signal of his brethren, he crawled to the door; and after the precaution of a Hebrew watchword, replied to in the same tongue, he gave admittance to the tall and stooping frame of the rich Elias.

"Worthy and excellent master," said Ximen, after again securing the entrance, "what can bring the honoured and wealthy Elias to the chamber of the poor hireling?"

"My friend," answered the Jew, "call me not wealthy nor honoured. For years I have dwelt within the city, safe and respected, even by the Moslemin, verily and because I have purchased, with jewels and treasure, the protection of the king and the great men. But now, alas! in the sudden wrath of the heathen — ever imagining vain things — I have been summoned into the presence of their chief rabbi, and only escaped the torture by a sum that ten years of labour and the sweat of my brow cannot replace. Ximen, the bitterest thought of all is that the frenzy of one of our own tribe has brought this desolation upon Israel."

"My lord speaks riddles," said Ximen, with well-feigned astonishment in his glassy eyes.

"Why dost thou wind and turn, good Ximen?" said the Jew, shaking his head. "Thou knowest well what my words drive at. Thy master is the pretended Almamen; and that recreant Israelite (if Israelite, indeed, still be one who hath forsaken the customs and the forms of his forefathers) is he who hath stirred up the Jews of Cordova and Guadix, and whose folly hath brought upon us these dread things. Holy Abraham! this Jew hath cost me more than fifty Nazarenes and a hundred Moors."

Ximen remained silent; and the tongue of Elias being loosed by the recollection of his sad loss, the latter continued: "At the first, when the son of Issachar reappeared and became a counsellor in the king's court, I indeed, who had led him, then a child, to the synagogue, — for old Issachar was to me dear as a brother, — recognized him by his eyes and voice. But I exulted in his craft and concealment; I believed he would work mighty things for his poor brethren, and would obtain for his father's friend the supplying of the king's wives and concubines with raiment and cloth of price. But years have passed: he hath not lightened our burdens; and by the madness that hath of late come over him, heading the heathen armies and drawing our brethren into danger and death, he hath deserved the curse of the synagogue and the wrath of our whole race. I find, from our brethren who escaped the Inquisition by the surrender of their substance,

that his unskilful and frantic schemes were the main pretext
for the sufferings of the righteous under the Nazarene; and,
again, the same schemes bring on us the same oppression
from the Moor. Accursed be he, and may his name perish!"

Ximen sighed, but remained silent, conjecturing to what
end the Jew would bring his invectives. He was not long in
suspense. After a pause, Elias recommenced, in an altered
and more careless tone: "He is rich, this son of Issachar, —
wondrous rich."

"He has treasures scattered over half the cities of Africa
and the Orient," said Ximen.

"Thou seest, then, my friend, that thy master hath doomed
me to a heavy loss. I possess his secret; I could give him
up to the king's wrath; I could bring him to the death. But
I am just and meek: let him pay my forfeiture, and I will
forego mine anger."

"Thou dost not know him," said Ximen, alarmed at the
thought of a repayment which might grievously diminish his
own heritage of Almamen's effects in Granada.

"But if I threaten him with exposure?"

"Thou wouldst feed the fishes of the Darro," interrupted
Ximen. "Nay, even now, if Almamen learn that thou knowest his birth and race, tremble; for thy days in the land will
be numbered."

"Verily," exclaimed the Jew, in great alarm, "then have I
fallen into the snare; for these lips revealed to him that
knowledge."

"Then is the righteous Elias a lost man, within ten days
from that in which Almamen returns to Granada. I know
my master, and blood is to him as water."

"Let the wicked be consumed!" cried Elias, furiously,
stamping his foot, while fire flashed from his dark eyes; for
the instinct of self-preservation made him fierce. "Not from
me, however," he added, more calmly, "will come his danger.
Know that there be more than a hundred Jews in this city
who have sworn his death, — Jews who, flying hither from
Cordova, have seen their parents murdered and their substance seized, and who behold in the son of Issachar the

*ause of the murder and the spoil. They have detected the impostor, and a hundred knives are whetting even now for his blood: let him look to it! Ximen, I have spoken to thee as the foolish speak, — thou mayest betray me to thy lord; but from what I have learned of thee from our brethren, I have poured my heart into thy bosom without fear. Wilt thou betray Israel, or assist us to smite the traitor?"

Ximen mused for a moment, and his meditation conjured up the treasures of his master. He stretched forth his right hand to Elias, and when the Israelites parted, they were friends.

CHAPTER VI.

BOABDIL'S RETURN. — THE REAPPEARANCE OF FERDINAND
BEFORE GRANADA.

THE third morning from this interview a rumour reached Granada that Boabdil had been repulsed in his assault on the citadel of Salobreña with a severe loss, that Hernando del Pulgar had succeeded in conducting to its relief a considerable force, and that the army of Ferdinand was on its march against the Moorish king. In the midst of the excitement occasioned by these reports a courier arrived to confirm their truth and to announce the return of Boabdil.

At nightfall the king, preceding his army, entered the city, and hastened to bury himself in the Alhambra. As he passed dejectedly into the women's apartments, his stern mother met him.

"My son," she said bitterly, "dost thou return, and not a conqueror?"

Before Boabdil could reply, a light and rapid step sped through the glittering arcades; and weeping with joy, and breaking all the Oriental restraints, Amine fell upon his bosom. "My beloved, my king, light of mine eyes, thou hast returned! Welcome; for thou art safe!"

The different form of these several salutations struck Boabdil forcibly. "Thou seest, my mother," said he, "how great the contrast between those who love us from affection, and those who love us from pride. In adversity, God keep me, O my mother, from thy tongue!"

"But I love thee from pride too," murmured Amine; "and for that reason is thine adversity dear to me, for it takes thee from the world to make thee more mine own. And I am proud of the afflictions that my hero shares with his slave."

"Lights there, and the banquet!" cried the king, turning from his haughty mother; "we will feast and be merry while we may. My adored Amine, kiss me!"

Proud, melancholy, and sensitive as he was in that hour of reverse, Boabdil felt no grief: such balm has Love for our sorrows, when its wings are borrowed from the dove! And although the laws of the Eastern life confined to the narrow walls of a harem the sphere of Amine's gentle influence; although, even in romance, THE NATURAL compels us to portray her vivid and rich colours only in a faint and hasty sketch,—yet still are left to the outline the loveliest and the noblest features of the sex: the spirit to arouse us to exertion, the softness to console us in our fall!

While Boabdil and the body of the army remained in the city, Muza, with a chosen detachment of the horse, scoured the country to visit the newly acquired cities and sustain their courage.

From this charge he was recalled by the army of Ferdinand, which once more poured down into the Vega, completely devastated its harvests, and then swept back to consummate the conquests of the revolted towns. To this irruption succeeded an interval of peace, — the calm before the storm. From every part of Spain the most chivalric and resolute of the Moors taking advantage of the pause in the contest, flocked to Granada; and that city became the focus of all that paganism in Europe possessed of brave and determined spirits.

At length Ferdinand, completing his conquests, and having refilled his treasury, mustered the whole force of his dominions, — forty thousand foot, and ten thousand horse, and once more, and for the last time, appeared before the walls of Granada. A solemn and prophetic determination filled both besiegers and besieged; each felt that the crowning crisis was at hand.

CHAPTER VII.

THE CONFLAGRATION. — THE MAJESTY OF AN INDIVIDUAL PASSION IN THE MIDST OF HOSTILE THOUSANDS.

It was the eve of a great and general assault upon Granada, deliberately planned by the chiefs of the Christian army. The Spanish camp (the most gorgeous Christendom had ever known) gradually grew calm and hushed. The shades deepened, the stars burned forth more serene and clear. Bright, in that azure air streamed the silken tents of the court, blazoned with heraldic devices and crowned by gaudy banners, which, filled by a brisk and murmuring wind from the mountains, flaunted gayly on their gilded staves. In the centre of the camp rose the pavilion of the queen, — a palace in itself. Lances made its columns; brocade and painted arras its walls; and the space covered by its numerous compartments would have contained the halls and outworks of an ordinary castle. The pomp of that camp realized the wildest dreams of Gothic coupled with Oriental splendour, — something worthy of a Tasso to have imagined, or a Beckford to create. Nor was the exceeding costliness of the more courtly tents lessened in effect by those of the soldiery in the outskirts, many of which were built from boughs still retaining their leaves, — savage and picturesque huts, — as if, realizing old legends, wild men of the woods had taken up the cross and followed the Christian warriors against the swarthy followers of Termagaunt and Mahound. There, then, extended that mighty camp in profound repose as the midnight threw deeper and longer shadows over the sward from the tented avenues and canvas streets. It was at that hour that Isabel, in the most private recess of her pavilion, was employed in prayer for the safety of the king and the issue of the Sacred War. Kneeling before the altar of that warlike oratory, her spirit became rapt and absorbed from earth in the intensity of her devotions; and in the whole camp (save the sentries), the eyes of that pious queen were perhaps the only ones unclosed. All was profoundly still; her guards, her attendants, were gone to rest; and the tread of the sentinel without that immense pavilion, was not heard through the silken walls.

It was then that Isabel suddenly felt a strong grasp upon her shoulder as she still knelt by the altar. A faint shriek burst from her lips; she turned, and the broad, curved knife of an Eastern warrior gleamed close before her eyes.

"Hush! utter a cry, breathe more loudly than thy wont, and, queen though thou art, in the centre of swarming thousands, thou diest!"

Such were the words that reached the ear of the royal Castilian, whispered by a man of stern and commanding, though haggard, aspect.

"What is thy purpose? Wouldst thou murder me?" said the queen, trembling, perhaps for the first time, before a mortal presence.

"Thy life is safe, if thou strivest not to delude or to deceive me. Our time is short, — answer me! I am Almamen the Hebrew. Where is the hostage rendered to thy hands? I claim my child. She is with thee, I know it. In what corner of thy camp?"

"Rude stranger!" said Isabel, recovering somewhat from her alarm, "thy daughter is removed, I trust forever, from thine impious reach. She is not within the camp."

"Lie not, Queen of Castile," said Almamen, raising his knife. "For days and weeks I have tracked thy steps, followed thy march, haunted even thy slumbers, though men of mail stood as guards around them; and I know that my daughter has been with thee. Think not I brave this danger without resolves the most fierce and dread. Answer me, where is my child?"

"Many days since," said Isabel, awed, despite herself, by her strange position, "thy daughter left the camp for the house of God. It was her own desire. The Saviour hath received her into his fold."

Had a thousand lances pierced his heart, the vigour and energy of life could scarce more suddenly have deserted Almamen. The rigid muscles of his countenance relaxed at once, from resolve and menace, into unutterable horror, anguish, and despair. He recoiled several steps; his knees trembled violently; he seemed stunned by a death-blow. Isabel, the boldest and haughtiest of her sex, seized that moment of reprieve; she sprang forward, darted through the draperies into the apartments occupied by her train, and in a moment the pavilion resounded with her cries for aid. The sentinels were aroused; retainers sprang from their pillows; they heard the cause of the alarm; they made to the spot: when, ere they reached its partition of silk, a vivid and startling blaze burst forth upon them. The tent was on fire. The materials fed the flame like magic. Some of the guards had yet the courage to dash forward, but the smoke and the glare drove them back, blinded and dizzy. Isabel herself had scarcely time for escape, so rapid was the conflagration. Alarmed for her husband, she rushed to his tent, — to find him already awakened by the noise, and issuing from its entrance, his drawn sword in his hand. The wind, which had a few minutes before but curled the triumphant banners, now circulated the destroying flame. It spread from tent to tent almost as a flash of lightning that shoots along neighbouring clouds. The camp was in one continued blaze ere any man could dream of checking the conflagration.

Not waiting to hear the confused tale of his royal consort, Ferdinand, exclaiming, "The Moors have done this; they will be on us!" ordered the drums to beat and the trumpets to sound, and hastened in person, wrapped merely in his long mantle, to alarm his chiefs. While that well-disciplined and veteran army, fearing every moment the rally of the foe, endeavoured rapidly to form themselves into some kind of order, the flame continued to spread till the whole heavens were illumined. By its light, cuirass and helmet glowed as in the furnace, and the armed men seemed rather like life-like and lurid meteors than human forms. The city of Granada was brought near to them by the intensity of the glow; and as a detachment of cavalry spurred from the camp to meet the anticipated surprise of the Paynims, they saw, upon the walls and roofs of Granada, the Moslems clustering, and their spears gleaming. But equally amazed with the Christians, and equally suspicious of craft and design, the Moors did not issue from their gates. Meanwhile the conflagration, as rapid to die as to begin, grew fitful and feeble, and the night seemed to fall with a melancholy darkness over the ruin of that silken city.

Ferdinand summoned his council. He had now perceived it was no ambush of the Moors. The account of Isabel, which at last he comprehended; the strange and almost miraculous manner in which Almamen had baffled his guards, and penetrated to the royal tent, — might have aroused his Gothic superstition, while it relieved his more earthly apprehensions, if he had not remembered the singular, but far from supernatural, dexterity with which Eastern warriors, and even robbers, continued then, as now, to elude the most vigilant precautions, and baffle the most wakeful guards; and it was evident that the fire which burned the camp of an army had been kindled merely to gratify the revenge or favour the escape of an individual. Shaking, therefore, from his kingly spirit the thrill of superstitious awe that the greatness of the disaster, when associated with the name of a sorcerer, at first occasioned, he resolved to make advantage out of misfortune itself. The excitement, the wrath, of the troops produced the temper most fit for action.

"And Heaven," said the king of Spain to his knights and chiefs, as they assembled round him, "has, in this conflagration, announced to the warriors of the Cross that henceforth their camp shall be the palaces of Granada! Woe to the Moslem with to-morrow's sun!"

Arms clanged, and swords leaped from their sheaths, as the Christian knights echoed the anathema: "WOE TO THE MOSLEM!"

BOOK V.

CHAPTER I.

THE day slowly dawned upon that awful night; and the Moors, still upon the battlements of Granada, beheld the whole army of Ferdinand on its march towards their walls. At a distance lay the wrecks of the blackened and smouldering camp; while before them, gaudy and glittering pennons waving, and trumpets sounding, came the exultant legions of the foe. The Moors could scarcely believe their senses. Fondly anticipating the retreat of the Christians, after so signal a disaster, the gay and dazzling spectacle of their march to the assault filled them with consternation and alarm.

While yet wondering and inactive, the trumpet of Boabdil was heard behind, and they beheld the Moorish king, at the head of his guards, emerging down the avenues that led to the gate. The sight restored and exhilarated the gazers; and when Boabdil halted in the space before the portals, the shout of twenty thousand warriors rose ominously to the ears of the advancing Christians.

"Men of Granada," said Boabdil, as soon as the deep and breathless silence had succeeded to that martial acclamation, "the advance of the enemy is to their destruction! In the fire of last night, the hand of Allah wrote their doom. Let us forth, each and all! We will leave our homes unguarded; our hearts shall be their wall! True that our numbers are thinned by famine and by slaughter, but enough of us are yet left for the redemption of Granada. Nor are the dead departed from us, — the dead fight with us; their souls animate our own. He who has lost a brother, becomes twice a man. On this battle we will set all. Liberty or chains! empire or exile! victory or death! Forward!"

He spoke, and gave the rein to his barb. It bounded forward and cleared the gloomy arch of the portals, and Boabdil el Chico was the first Moor who issued from Granada to that last and eventful field. Out, then, poured, as a river that rushes from caverns into day, the burnished and serried files of the Moorish cavalry. Muza came the last, closing the array. Upon his dark and stern countenance there spoke not the ardent enthusiasm of the sanguine king. It was locked and rigid; and the anxieties of the last dismal weeks had thinned his cheeks, and ploughed deep lines around the firm lips and iron jaw which bespoke the obstinate and unconquerable resolution of his character.

As Muza now spurred forward, and, riding along the wheeling ranks, marshalled them in order, arose the acclamation of female voices; and the warriors, who looked back at the sound, saw that their women — their wives and daughters, their mothers and their beloved (released from their seclusion by a policy which bespoke the desperation of the cause) — were gazing at them, with outstretched arms, from the battlements and towers. The Moors knew that they were now to fight for their hearths and altars in the presence of those who, if they failed, became slaves and harlots; and each Moslem felt his heart harden like the steel of his own sabre.

While the cavalry formed themselves into regular squadrons, and the tramp of the foemen came more near and near, the Moorish infantry, in miscellaneous, eager, and undisciplined bands, poured out, until, spreading wide and deep below the walls, Boabdil's charger was seen, rapidly careering amongst them, as, in short but distinct directions or fiery adjuration, he sought at once to regulate their movements and confirm their hot but capricious valour.

Meanwhile the Christians had abruptly halted; and the politic Ferdinand resolved not to incur the full brunt of a whole population in the first flush of their enthusiasm and despair. He summoned to his side Hernando del Pulgar, and bade him, with a troop of the most adventurous and practised horsemen, advance towards the Moorish cavalry and endeavour to draw the fiery valour of Muza away from the main army. Then, splitting up his force into several sections, he dismissed each to different stations, — some to storm the adjacent towers, others to fire the surrounding gardens and orchards; so that the action might consist rather of many battles than of one, and the Moors might lose the concentration and union which made, at present, their most formidable strength.

Thus, while the Mussulmans were waiting in order for the attack, they suddenly beheld the main body of the Chrsitians dispersing; and while yet in surprise and perplexed, they saw the fires breaking out from their delicious gardens, to the right and left of the walls, and heard the boom of the Christian artillery against the scattered bulwarks that guarded the approaches of the city.

At that moment a cloud of dust rolled rapidly towards the post occupied in the van by Muza, and the shock of the Christian knights, in their mighty mail, broke upon the centre of the prince's squadron.

Higher by several inches than the plumage of his companions, waved the crest of the gigantic Del Pulgar; and as Moor after Moor went down before his headlong lance, his voice, sounding deep and sepulchral through his visor, shouted out: "Death to the infidel!"

The rapid and dexterous horsemen of Granada were not, however, discomfited by this fierce assault; opening their ranks with extraordinary celerity, they suffered the charge to pass, comparatively harmless, through their centre, and then, closing in one long and bristling line, cut off the knights from retreat. The Christians wheeled round, and charged again upon their foe.

"Where art thou, O Moslem dog that wouldst play the lion? Where art thou, Muza Ben Abil Gazan?"

"Before thee, Christian!" cried a stern and clear voice; and from amongst the helmets of his people gleamed the dazzling turban of the Moor.

Hernando checked his steed, gazed a moment at his foe, turned back, for greater impetus to his charge, and in a moment more the bravest warriors of the two armies met, lance to lance.

The round shield of Muza received the Christian's weapon; his own spear shivered, harmless, upon the breast of the giant. He drew his sword, whirled it rapidly over his head, and for some minutes the eyes of the bystanders could scarcely mark the marvellous rapidity with which strokes were given and parried by those redoubted swordsmen.

At length Hernando, anxious to bring to bear his superior strength, spurred close to Muza, and leaving his sword pendant by a thong to his wrist, seized the shield of Muza in his formidable grasp, and plucked it away, with a force that the Moor vainly endeavoured to resist; Muza therefore suddenly released his hold, and ere the Spaniard had recovered his balance (which was lost by the success of his own strength, put forth to the utmost), he dashed upon him the hoofs of his black charger, and with a short but heavy mace, which he caught up from the saddle-bow, dealt Hernando so thundering a blow upon the helmet that the giant fell to the ground stunned and senseless.

To dismount, to repossess himself of his shield, to resume his sabre, to put one knee to the breast of his fallen foe, was the work of a moment; and then had Don Hernando del Pulgar been sped, without priest or surgeon, but that, alarmed by the peril of their most valiant comrade, twenty knights spurred at once to the rescue, and the points of twenty lances kept the Lion of Granada from his prey. Thither, with similar speed, rushed the Moorish champions; and the fight became close and deadly round the body of the still unconscious Christian. Not an instant of leisure to unlace the helmet of Hernando, by removing which, alone, the Moorish blade could find a mortal place, was permitted to Muza; and what with the spears and trampling hoofs around him, the situation of the Paynim was more dangerous than that of the Christian. Meanwhile, Hernando recovered his dizzy senses; and, made aware of his state, watched his occasion and suddenly shook off the knee of the Moor. With another effort he was on his feet, and the two champions stood confronting each other, neither very eager to renew the combat. But on foot Muza, daring and rash as he was, could not but recognize his disadvantage against the enormous strength and impenetrable armour of the Christian. He drew back, whistled to his barb, that, piercing the ranks of the horsemen, was by his side on the instant, remounted, and was in the midst of the foe almost ere the slower Spaniard was conscious of his disappearance.

But Hernando was not delivered from his enemy. Clearing a space around him, as three knights, mortally wounded, fell beneath his sabre, Muza now drew from behind his shoulder his short Arabian bow, and shaft after shaft came rattling upon the mail of the dismounted Christian with so marvellous a celerity that, encumbered as he was with his heavy accoutrements, he was unable either to escape from the spot or ward off that arrowy rain, and felt that nothing but chance or our Lady could prevent the death which one such arrow would occasion, if it should find the opening of the visor or the joints of the hauberk.

"Mother of Mercy," groaned the knight, perplexed and enraged, "let not thy servant be shot down like a hart by this cowardly warfare, but if I must fall, be it with mine enemy, grappling hand to hand."

While yet muttering this short invocation, the war-cry of Spain was heard hard by, and the gallant company of Villena was seen scouring across the plain to the succour of their comrades. The deadly attention of Muza was distracted from individual foes, however eminent; he wheeled round, re-collected his men, and in a serried charge met the new enemy in midway.

While the contest thus fared in that part of the field, the scheme of Ferdinand had succeeded so far as to break up the battle in detached sections. Far and near, plain, grove, garden, tower, presented each the scene of obstinate and determined conflict. Boabdil, at the head of his chosen guard, — the flower of the haughtier tribe of nobles who were jealous of the fame and blood of the tribe of Muza, — and followed also by his gigantic Ethiopians, exposed his person to every peril with the desperate valour of a man who feels his own stake is greatest in the field. As he most distrusted the infantry, so amongst the infantry he chiefly bestowed his presence; and wherever he appeared, he sufficed, for the moment, to turn the changes of the engagement. At length, at mid-day, Ponce de Leon led against the largest detachment of the Moorish foot a strong and numerous battalion of the best-disciplined and veteran soldiery of Spain. He had succeeded in winning a fortress from which his artillery could play with effect; and the troops he led were composed partly of men flushed with recent triumph, and partly of a fresh reserve, now first brought into the field. A comely and a breathless spectacle it was to behold this Christian squadron emerging from a blazing copse, which they fired on their march, the red light gleaming on their complete armour as, in steady and solemn order, they swept on to the swaying and clamorous ranks of the Moorish infantry. Boabdil learned the danger from his scouts; and hastily quitting a tower from which he had for a while repulsed a hostile legion, he threw himself into the midst of the battalions menaced by the skilful Ponce de Leon. Almost at the same moment the wild and ominous apparition of Almamen, long absent from the eyes of the Moors, appeared in the same quarter, so suddenly and unexpectedly that none knew whence he had emerged; the sacred standard in his left hand, his sabre, bared and dripping gore, in his right, his face exposed, and its powerful features working with an excitement that seemed inspired, his abrupt presence breathed a new soul into the Moors.

"They come, they come!" he shrieked aloud. "The God of the East hath delivered the Goth into your hands!"

From rank to rank, from line to line, sped the santon; and as the mystic banner gleamed before the soldiery, each closed his eyes and muttered an "amen" to his adjurations.

And now to the cry of "Spain and Saint Iago" came trampling down the relentless charge of the Christian war.

At the same instant, from the fortress lately taken by Ponce de Leon the artillery opened upon the Moors and did deadly havoc. The Moslems wavered a moment when before them gleamed the white banner of Almamen; and they beheld him rushing, alone and on foot, amidst the foe. Taught to believe the war itself depended on the preservation of the enchanted banner, the Paynims could not see it thus rashly adventured without anxiety and shame; they rallied, advanced firmly, and Boabdil himself, with waving cimeter and fierce exclamations, dashed impetuously at the head of his guards and Ethiopians into the affray. The battle became obstinate and bloody. Thrice the white banner disappeared amidst the closing ranks, and thrice, like a moon from the clouds, it shone forth again, — the light and guide of the Pagan power.

The day ripened, and the hills already cast lengthening shadows over the blazing groves and the still Darro, whose waters, in every creek where the tide was arrested, ran red with blood, when Ferdinand, collecting his whole reserve, descended from the eminence on which hitherto he had posted himself. With him moved three thousand foot and a thousand horse, fresh in their vigour, and panting for a share in that glorious day. The king himself, who, though constitutionally fearless, from motives of policy rarely perilled his person save on imminent occasions, was resolved not to be outdone by Boabdil; and armed *cap-a-pie* in mail, so wrought with gold that it seemed nearly all of that costly metal, with his snow-white plumage waving above a small diadem that surmounted his lofty helm, he seemed a fit leader to that armament of heroes. Behind him flaunted the great gonfalon of Spain, and trump and cymbal heralded his approach. The Count de Tendilla rode by his side.

"Señor," said Ferdinand, "the infidels fight hard; but they are in the snare, — we are about to close the nets upon them. But what cavalcade is this?"

The group that thus drew the king's attention consisted of six squires, bearing, on a martial litter composed of shields, the stalwart form of Hernando del Pulgar.

"Ah, the dogs!" cried the king, as he recognized the pale

features of the darling of the army, — "have they murdered the bravest knight that ever fought for Christendom?"

"Not that, your Majesty," quoth he of the Exploits, faintly, "but I am sorely stricken."

"It must have been more than man who struck thee down," said the king.

"It was the mace of Muza Ben Abil Gazan, an please you, sire," said one of the squires; "but it came on the good knight unawares, and long after his own arm had seemingly driven away the Pagan."

"We will avenge thee well," said the king, setting his teeth; "let our own leeches tend thy wounds. Forward, sir knights! Saint Iago and Spain!"

The battle had now gathered to a vortex; Muza and his cavalry had joined Boabdil and the Moorish foot. On the other hand, Villena had been reinforced by detachments that in almost every other quarter of the field had routed the foe. The Moors had been driven back, though inch by inch; they were now in the broad space before the very walls of the city, which were still crowded by the pale and anxious faces of the aged and the women; and at every pause in the artillery, the voices that spoke of HOME were borne by that lurid air to the ears of the infidels. The shout that rang through the Christian force as Ferdinand now joined it struck like a death-knell upon the last hope of Boabdil. But the blood of his fierce ancestry burned in his veins, and the cheering voice of Almamen, whom nothing daunted, inspired him with a kind of superstitious frenzy.

"King against king, — so be it! Let Allah decide between us!" cried the Moorish monarch. "Bind up this wound, — 't is well! A steed for the santon! Now, my prophet and my friend, mount by the side of thy king; let us at least fall together. Lelilies! Lelilies!"

Throughout the brave Christian ranks went a thrill of reluctant admiration as they beheld the Paynim king, conspicuous by his fair beard and the jewels of his harness, lead the scanty guard yet left to him once more into the thickest of their lines. Simultaneously Muza and his Zegris made their fiery charge; and the Moorish infantry, excited by the example of their leaders, followed with unslackened and dogged zeal. The Christians gave way, — they were beaten back; Ferdinand spurred forward; and ere either party were well aware of it, both kings met in the same *mêlée*. All order and discipline for the moment lost, general and monarch were, as common soldiers, fighting hand to hand. It was then that Ferdinand, after bearing down before his lance Naim Reduon, second only to Muza in the songs of Granada, beheld opposed to him a strange form that seemed to that royal Christian rather fiend than man; his raven hair and beard, clotted with blood, hung like snakes about a countenance whose features, naturally formed to give expression to the darkest passions, were distorted with the madness of despairing rage. Wounded in many places, the blood dabbled his mail, while over his head he waved the banner wrought with mystic characters, which Ferdinand had already been taught to believe the workmanship of demons.

"Now, perjured king of the Nazarenes," shouted this formidable champion, "we meet at last, no longer host and guest, monarch and dervise, but man to man! I am Almamen! Die!"

He spoke; and his sword descended so fiercely on that anointed head that Ferdinand bent to his saddle-bow. But the king quickly recovered his seat, and gallantly met the encounter: it was one that might have tasked to the utmost the prowess of his bravest knight. Passions which in their number, their nature, and their excess animated no other champion on either side, gave to the arm of Almamen the Israelite a preternatural strength; his blows fell like rain upon the harness of the king; and the fiery eyes, the gleaming banner of the mysterious sorcerer who had eluded the tortures of his Inquisition, who had walked unscathed through the midst of his army, whose single hand had consumed the encampment of a host, filled the stout heart of the king with a belief that he encountered no earthly foe. Fortunately, perhaps, for Ferdinand and Spain, the contest did not last long. Twenty horsemen spurred into the *mêlée* to the rescue of the plumed diadem. Tendilla arrived the first; with a stroke of his two-handed sword, the white banner was cleft from its staff and fell to the earth. At that sight the Moors round broke forth in a wild and despairing cry; that cry spread from rank to rank, from horse to foot. The Moorish infantry, sorely pressed on all sides, no sooner learned the disaster than they turned to fly: the rout was as fatal as it was sudden. The Christian reserve, just brought into the field, poured down upon them with a simultaneous charge. Boabdil, too much engaged to be the first to learn the downfall of the sacred insignia, suddenly saw himself almost alone, with his diminished Ethiopians and a handful of his cavaliers.

"Yield thee, Boabdil el Chico!" cried Tendilla from his rear, "or thou canst not be saved."

"By the Prophet, never!" exclaimed the king; and he dashed his barb against the wall of spears behind him, and with but a score or so of his guard cut his way through the ranks that were not unwilling, perhaps, to spare so brave a foe. As he cleared the Spanish battalions, the unfortunate monarch checked his horse for a moment and gazed along the plain: he beheld his army flying in all directions, save in that single spot where yet glittered the turban of Muza Ben Abil Gazan. As he gazed, he heard the panting nostrils of the chargers behind, and saw the levelled spears of a company despatched to take him, alive or dead, by the command of Ferdinand. He laid the reins upon his horse's neck and galloped into the city: three lances quivered against the portals as he disappeared through the shadows of the arch. But while Muza remained, all was not yet lost; he perceived the flight of the infantry and the king, and with his followers galloped across the plain. He came in time to encounter and slay, to a man, the pursuers of Boabdil; he then threw himself before the flying Moors.

"Do ye fly in the sight of your wives and daughters? Would ye not rather they beheld you die?"

A thousand voices answered him: "The banner is in the hands of the infidel, — all is lost!" They swept by him, and stopped not till they gained the gates.

But still a small and devoted remnant of the Moorish cavaliers remained to shed a last glory over defeat itself. With Muza, their soul and centre, they fought every atom of ground; it was, as the chronicler expresses it, as if they grasped ... soil with their arms. Twice they charged into the midst of the foe; the slaughter they made, doubled their own number. But gathering on and closing in, squadron upon squadron, came the whole Christian army; they were encompassed, wearied out, beaten back, as by an ocean. Like wild beasts driven at length to their lair, they retreated with their faces to the foe; and when Muza came, the last, — his cimeter shivered to the hilt, — he had scarcely breath to command the gates to be closed and the portcullis lowered, ere he fell from his charger in a sudden and deadly swoon, caused less by his exhaustion than his agony and shame. So ended the last battle fought for the Monarchy of Granada.

CHAPTER II.

THE NOVICE.

It was in one of the cells of a convent renowned for the piety of its inmates and the wholesome austerity of its laws that a young novice sat alone. The narrow casement was placed so high in the cold gray wall as to forbid to the tenant of the cell the solace of sad or the distraction of pious thoughts, which a view of the world without might afford. Lovely indeed was the landscape that spread below, but it was barred from those youthful and melancholy eyes; for Nature might tempt to a thousand thoughts not of a tenor calculated to reconcile the heart to an eternal sacrifice of the sweet human ties. But a faint and partial gleam of sunshine broke through the aperture, and made yet more cheerless the dreary aspect and gloomy appurtenances of the cell; and the young novice seemed to carry on within herself that struggle of emotions

without which there is no victory in the resolves of virtue.
Sometimes she wept bitterly, but with a low, subdued sorrow
which spoke rather of despondency than passion; sometimes
she raised her head from her breast and smiled as she looked
upward, or as her eyes rested on the crucifix and the death's
head that were placed on the rude table by the pallet on
which she sat. They were emblems of death here, and life
hereafter, which perhaps afforded to her the sources of a two-
fold consolation.

She was yet musing when a slight tap at the door was
heard, and the abbess of the convent appeared.

"Daughter," said she, "I have brought thee the comfort of
a sacred visitor. The Queen of Spain, whose pious tenderness is maternally anxious for thy full contentment with thy
lot, has sent hither a holy friar whom she deems more soothing in his counsels than our brother Tomas, whose ardent zeal
often terrifies those whom his honest spirit only desires to
purify and guide. I will leave him with thee. May the
saints bless his ministry!" So saying, the abbess retired
from the threshold, making way for a form in the garb of a
monk, with the hood drawn over the face. The monk bowed
his head meekly, advanced into the cell, closed the door, and
seated himself on a stool which, save the table and the pallet,
seemed the sole furniture of the dismal chamber.

"Daughter," said he, after a pause, "it is a rugged and a
mournful lot, this renunciation of earth and all its fair destinies and soft affections, to one not wholly prepared and
armed for the sacrifice. Confide in me, my child; I am no
dire Inquisitor, seeking to distort thy words to thine own
peril. I am no bitter and morose ascetic. Beneath these
robes still beats a human heart that can sympathize with
human sorrows. Confide in me without fear. Dost thou not
dread the fate they would force upon thee? Dost thou not
shrink back? Wouldst thou not be free?"

"No," said the poor novice; but the denial came faint and
irresolute from her lips.

"Pause," said the friar, growing more earnest in his tone;
"pause, — there is yet time."

"Nay," said the novice, looking up with some surprise in her countenance, — "nay, even were I so weak, escape now is impossible. What hand could unbar the gates of the convent?"

"Mine!" cried the monk, with impetuosity. "Yes, I have that power. In all Spain, but one man can save thee, and I am he."

"You!" faltered the novice, gazing at her strange visitor with mingled astonishment and alarm. "And who are you that could resist the fiat of that Tomas de Torquemada before whom, they tell me, even the crowned heads of Castile and Arragon veil low?"

The monk half rose, with an impatient and almost haughty start, at this interrogatory; but reseating himself, replied, in a deep and half-whispered voice: "Daughter, listen to me! It is true that Isabel of Spain (whom the Mother of Mercy bless; for merciful to all is her secret heart, if not her outward policy), — it is true that Isabel of Spain, fearful that the path to heaven might be made rougher to thy feet than it well need be [there was a slight accent of irony in the monk's voice as he thus spoke], selected a friar of suasive eloquence and gentle manners to visit thee. He was charged with letters to yon abbess from the queen. Soft though the friar, he was yet a hypocrite. — Nay, hear me out! — He loved to worship the rising sun; and he did not wish always to remain a simple friar, while the Church had higher dignities of this earth to bestow. In the Christian camp, daughter, there was one who burned for tidings of thee, — whom thine image haunted; who, stern as thou wert to him, loved thee with a love he knew not of, till thou wert lost to him. Why dost thou tremble, daughter? Listen, yet! To that lover — for he was one of high birth — came the monk; to that lover the monk sold his mission. The monk will have a ready tale, that he was waylaid amidst the mountains by armed men, and robbed of his letters to the abbess. The lover took his garb, and he took the letters, and he hastened hither. Leila, beloved Leila, behold him at thy feet!"

The monk raised his cowl, and dropping on his knee be-

side her, presented to her gaze the features of the Prince of
Spain.

"You!" said Leila, averting her countenance, and vainly
endeavouring to extricate the hand which he had seized.
"This is indeed cruel. You, the author of so many sufferings, such calumny, such reproach!"

"I will repair all," said Don Juan, fervently. "I alone—
I repeat it—have the power to set you free. You are no
longer a Jewess,—you are one of our faith; there is now no
bar upon our loves. Imperious though my father, all dark
and dread as is this new POWER which he is rashly erecting
in his dominions, the heir of two monarchies is not so poor in
influence and in friends as to be unable to offer the woman of
his love an inviolable shelter alike from priest and despot.
Fly with me; quit this dreary sepulchre ere the last stone
close over thee forever! I have horses, I have guards at
hand. This night it can be arranged. This night—oh,
bliss!—thou mayest be rendered up to earth and love!"

"Prince," said Leila, who had drawn herself from Juan's
grasp during this address, and who now stood at a little distance, erect and proud, "you tempt me in vain; or, rather,
you offer me no temptation. I have made my choice,—I
abide by it."

"Oh, bethink thee," said the prince, in a voice of real and
imploring anguish, —"bethink thee well of the consequences
of thy refusal! Thou canst not see them yet; thine ardour
blinds thee. But when hour after hour, day after day, year
after year, steals on in the appalling monotony of this sancti-
fied prison; when thou shalt see thy youth withering without
love, thine age without honour; when thy heart shall grow as
stone within thee, beneath the looks of yon icy spectres; when
nothing shall vary the aching dulness of wasted life save a
longer fast or a severer penance, —then, then will thy grief
be rendered tenfold by the despairing and remorseful thought
that thine own lips sealed thine own sentence. Thou mayest
think," continued Juan, with rapid eagerness, "that my love
to thee was at first light and dishonouring. Be it so. I own
that my youth has passed in idle wooings and the mockeries

of affection. But for the first time in my life I feel that *I love*. Thy dark eyes, thy noble beauty, even thy womanly scorn, have fascinated me. I — never yet disdained where I have been a suitor — acknowledge at last that there is a triumph in the conquest of a woman's heart. Oh, Leila! do not, do not reject me. You know not how rare and how deep a love you cast away."

The novice was touched. The present language of Don Juan was so different from what it had been before; the earnest love that breathed in his voice, that looked from his eyes, struck a chord in her breast, — it reminded her of her own unconquered, unconquerable love for the lost Muza. She was touched, then, — touched to tears; but her resolves were not shaken.

"Oh, Leila!" resumed the prince, fondly, mistaking the nature of her emotion, and seeking to pursue the advantage he imagined he had gained, "look at yonder sunbeam, struggling through the loophole of thy cell. Is it not a messenger from the happy world? Does it not plead for me? Does it not whisper to thee of the green fields, and the laughing vineyards, and all the beautiful prodigality of that earth thou art about to renounce forever? Dost thou dread my love? Are the forms around thee, ascetic and lifeless, fairer to thine eyes than mine? Dost thou doubt my power to protect thee? I tell thee that the proudest nobles of Spain would flock around my banner, were it necessary to guard thee by force of arms. Yet, speak the word, be mine, and I will fly hence with thee to climes where the Church has not cast out its deadly roots, and, forgetful of crowns and cares, live alone for thee. Ah, speak!"

"My lord," said Leila, calmly, and rousing herself to the necessary effort, "I am deeply and sincerely grateful for the interest you express, for the affection you avow. But you deceive yourself. I have pondered well over the alternative I have taken. I do not regret nor repent, much less would I retract it. The earth that you speak of, full of affections and of bliss to others, has no ties, no allurements for me. I desire only peace, repose, and an early death."

"Can it be possible," said the prince, growing pale, "that thou lovest another? Then, indeed, and then only would my wooing be in vain."

The cheek of the novice grew deeply flushed, but the colour soon subsided. She murmured to herself, "Why should I blush to own it now?" and then spoke aloud: "Prince, I trust I have done with the world; and bitter the pang I feel when you call me back to it. But you merit my candour: I *have* loved another; and in that thought, as in an urn, lie the ashes of all affection. That other is of a different faith. We may never, never meet again below; but it is a solace to pray that we may meet above. That solace and these cloisters are dearer to me than all the pomp, all the pleasures, of the world."

The prince sank down, and covering his face with his hands, groaned aloud, but made no reply.

"Go, then, Prince of Spain," continued the novice; "son of the noble Isabel, Leila is not unworthy of her cares. Go, and pursue the great destinies that await you. And if you forgive — if you still cherish a thought of — the poor Jewish maiden, soften, alleviate, mitigate, the wretched and desperate doom that awaits the fallen race she has abandoned for thy creed."

"Alas, alas!" said the prince, mournfully, "thee alone, perchance, of all thy race I could have saved from the bigotry that is fast covering this knightly land like the rising of an irresistible sea, — and thou rejectest me! Take time, at least, to pause, to consider. Let me see thee again to-morrow."

"No, prince, no; not again! I will keep thy secret only if I see thee no more. If thou persist in a suit that I feel to be that of sin and shame, then, indeed, mine honour — "

"Hold!" interrupted Juan, with haughty impatience, — "I torment, I harass you no more. I release you from my importunity. Perhaps already I have stooped too low." He drew the cowl over his features and strode sullenly to the door; but turning for one last gaze on the form that had so strangely fascinated a heart capable of generous emotions, — the meek and despondent posture of the novice, her tender youth, her gloomy fate, melted his momentary pride and resentment. "God bless and reconcile thee, poor child!" he said, in a voice choked with contending passions; and the door closed upon his form.

"I thank thee, Heaven, that it was not Muza!" muttered Leila, breaking from a revery in which she seemed to be communing with her own soul; "I feel that I could not have resisted *him*." With that thought she knelt down, in humble and penitent self-reproach, and prayed for strength.

Ere she had risen from her supplications, her solitude was again invaded by Torquemada, the Dominican.

This strange man, though the author of cruelties at which nature recoils, had some veins of warm and gentle feeling streaking, as it were, the marble of his hard character; and when he had thoroughly convinced himself of the pure and earnest zeal of the young convert, he relaxed from the grim sternness he had at first exhibited towards her. He loved to exert the eloquence he possessed, in raising her spirit, in reconciling her doubts. He prayed *for* her, and he prayed *beside* her, with passion and with tears.

He stayed long with the novice, and when he left her, she was, if not happy, at least contented. Her warmest wish now was to abridge the period of her novitiate, which, at her desire, the Church had already rendered merely a nominal probation. She longed to put irresolution out of her power, and to enter at once upon the narrow road through the strait gate.

The gentle and modest piety of the young novice touched the sisterhood; she was endeared to all of them. Her conversion was an event that broke the lethargy of their stagnant life. She became an object of general interest, of avowed pride, of kindly compassion; and their kindness to her, who from her cradle had seen little of her own sex, had a great effect towards calming and soothing her mind. But at night her dreams brought before her the dark and menacing countenance of her father. Sometimes he seemed to pluck her from the gates of heaven, and to sink with her into the yawning abyss below. Sometimes she saw him with her beside the altar, but imploring her to forswear the Saviour before whose crucifix she knelt. Occasionally her visions were haunted, also, with Muza, but in less terrible guise. She saw his calm and melancholy eyes fixed upon her; and his voice asked, "Canst thou take a vow that makes it sinful to remember me?"

The night, that usually brings balm and oblivion to the sad, was thus made more dreadful to Leila than the day. Her health grew feebler and feebler, but her mind still was firm. In happier time and circumstance that poor novice would have been a great character; but she was one of the countless victims the world knows not of, whose virtues are in silent motives, whose struggles are in the solitary heart.

Of the prince she heard and saw no more. There were times when she fancied, from oblique and obscure hints, that the Dominican had been aware of Don Juan's disguise and visit. But if so, that knowledge appeared only to increase the gentleness, almost the respect, which Torquemada manifested towards her. Certainly, since that day, from some cause or other, the priest's manner had been softened when he addressed her; and he, who seldom had recourse to other arts than those of censure and of menace, often uttered sentiments half of pity and half of praise.

Thus consoled and supported in the day, thus haunted and terrified by night, but still not repenting her resolve, Leila saw the time glide on to that eventful day when her lips were to pronounce that irrevocable vow which is the epitaph of life. While in this obscure and remote convent progressed the history of an individual, we are summoned back to witness the crowning fate of an expiring dynasty.

CHAPTER III.

THE PAUSE BETWEEN DEFEAT AND SURRENDER.

THE unfortunate Boabdil plunged once more amidst the recesses of the Alhambra. Whatever his anguish or his despondency, none were permitted to share, or even to witness, his emotions. But he especially resisted the admission to his solitude, demanded by his mother, implored by his faithful Amine, and sorrowfully urged by Muza; those most loved or most respected were, above all, the persons from whom he most shrank.

Almamen was heard of no more. It was believed that he had perished in the battle. But he was one of those who, precisely as they are effective when present, are forgotten in absence. And in the mean while, as the Vega was utterly desolated, and all supplies were cut off, famine, daily made more terrifically severe, diverted the attention of each humbler Moor from the fall of the city to his individual sufferings.

New persecutions fell upon the miserable Jews. Not having taken any share in the conflict (as was to be expected from men who had no stake in the country which they dwelt in, and whose brethren had been taught so severe a lesson upon the folly of interference), no sentiment of fellowship in danger mitigated the hatred and loathing with which they were held; and as, in their lust of gain, many of them continued, amidst the agony and starvation of the citizens, to sell food at enormous prices, the excitement of the multitude against them — released by the state of the city from all restraint and law — made itself felt by the most barbarous excesses. Many of the houses of the Israelites were attacked by the mob, plundered, razed to the ground, and the owners tortured to death, to extort confession of imaginary wealth. Not to sell what was demanded was a crime; to sell it was a crime also. These

miserable outcasts fled to whatever secret places the vaults of
their houses or the caverns in the hills within the city could
yet afford them, cursing their fate, and almost longing even
for the yoke of the Christian bigots.

Thus passed several days; the defence of the city was
abandoned to its naked walls and mighty gates. The glaring
sun looked down upon closed shops and depopulated streets,
save when some ghostly and skeleton band of the famished
poor collected, in a sudden paroxysm of revenge or despair,
around the stormed and fired mansion of a detested Israelite.

At length Boabdil aroused himself from his seclusion, and
Muza, to his own surprise, was summoned to the presence of
the king. He found Boabdil in one of the most gorgeous
halls of his gorgeous palace.

Within the Tower of Comares is a vast chamber, still called
the Hall of the Ambassadors. Here it was that Boabdil now
held his court. On the glowing walls hung trophies and
banners, and here and there an Arabian portrait of some
bearded king. By the windows, which overlooked the most
lovely banks of the Darro, gathered the santons and alfaquis,
a little apart from the main crowd. Beyond, through half-
veiling draperies, might be seen the great court of the
Alberca, whose peristyles were hung with flowers; while in
the centre, the gigantic basin, which gives its name to the
court, caught the sunlight obliquely, and its waves glittered
on the eye from amidst the roses that then clustered over it.

In the audience hall itself, a canopy, over the royal
cushions on which Boabdil reclined, was blazoned with the
heraldic insignia of Granada's monarchs. His guard and his
mutes and his eunuchs and his courtiers and his counsellors
and his captains were ranged in long files on either side the
canopy. It seemed the last flicker of the lamp of the Moorish
empire, that hollow and unreal pomp! As Muza approached
the monarch, he was startled by the change of his countenance: the young and beautiful Boabdil seemed to have
grown suddenly old; his eyes were sunken, his countenance
was sown with wrinkles, and his voice sounded broken and
hollow on the ears of his kinsman.

ENTRANCE TO THE HALL OF THE AMBASSADORS.

"Come hither, Muza," said he; "seat thyself beside me
and listen as thou best canst to the tidings we are about to
hear."

As Muza placed himself on a cushion a little below the
king, Boabdil motioned to one amongst the crowd.

"Hamet," said he, "thou hast examined the state of the
Christian camp: what news dost thou bring?"

"Light of the Faithful," answered the Moor, "it is a camp
no longer, — it has already become a city. Nine towns of
Spain were charged with the task. Stone has taken the place
of canvas; towers and streets arise like the buildings of a
genius; and the misbelieving king hath sworn that this new
city shall not be left until Granada sees his standard on its
walls."

"Go on," said Boabdil, calmly.

"Traders and men of merchandise flock thither daily; the
spot is one bazaar; all that should supply our famishing
country pours its plenty into their mart."

Boabdil motioned to the Moor to withdraw, and an alfaqui
advanced in his stead.

"Successor of the Prophet and darling of the world!" said
the reverend man, "the alfaquis and seers of Granada implore
thee on their knees to listen to their voice. They have consulted the Books of Fate; they have implored a sign from the
Prophet; and they find that the glory has left thy people and
thy crown. The fall of Granada is predestined. God is
great!"

"You shall have my answer forthwith," said Boabdil.
"Abdelmelic, approach."

From the crowd came an aged and white-bearded man, the
governor of the city.

"Speak, old man," said the king.

"Oh, Boabdil!" said the veteran, with faltering tones,
while the tears rolled down his cheeks, "son of a race of
kings and heroes! would that thy servant had fallen dead on
thy threshold this day, and that the lips of a Moorish noble
had never been polluted by the words that I now utter! Our
state is hopeless; our granaries are as the sands of the desert;

there is in them life neither for beast nor man. The war-horse that bore the hero is now consumed for his food; the population of thy city with one voice cry for chains and — bread! I have spoken."

"Admit the ambassador of Egypt," said Boabdil, as Abdelmelic retired. There was a pause. One of the draperies at the end of the hall was drawn aside, and with the slow and sedate majesty of their tribe and land, paced forth a dark and swarthy train, the envoys of the Egyptian soldan. Six of the band bore costly presents of gems and weapons, and the procession closed with four veiled slaves, whose beauty had been the boast of the ancient valley of the Nile.

"Sun of Granada and day-star of the faithful," said the chief of the Egyptians, "my lord, the soldan of Egypt, delight of the world and rose-tree of the East, thus answers to the letters of Boabdil. He grieves that he cannot send the succour thou demandest; and informing himself of the condition of thy territories, he finds that Granada no longer holds a seaport by which his forces (could he send them) might find an entrance into Spain. He implores thee to put thy trust in Allah, who will not desert his chosen ones, and lays these gifts, in pledge of amity and love, at the feet of my lord the king."

"It is a gracious and well-timed offering," said Boabdil, with a writhing lip; "we thank him."

There was now a long and dead silence as the ambassadors swept from the hall of audience, when Boabdil suddenly raised his head from his breast and looked around his hall with a kingly and majestic look. "Let the heralds of Ferdinand of Spain approach."

A groan involuntarily broke from the breast of Muza. It was echoed by a murmur of abhorrence and despair from the gallant captains who stood around; but to that momentary burst succeeded a breathless silence as from another drapery, opposite the royal couch, gleamed the burnished mail of the knights of Spain. Foremost of these haughty visitors, whose iron heels clanked loudly on the tessellated floor, came a noble and stately form in full armour, save the helmet, and with a mantle of azure velvet, wrought with the silver cross that made the badge of the Christian war. Upon his manly countenance was visible no sign of undue arrogance or exultation, but something of that generous pity which brave men feel for conquered foes dimmed the lustre of his commanding eye, and softened the wonted sternness of his martial bearing. He and his train approached the king with a profound salutation of respect; and falling back, motioned to the herald that accompanied him, and whose garb, breast and back, was wrought with the arms of Spain, to deliver himself of his mission.

"To Boabdil," said the herald, with a loud voice, that filled the whole expanse and thrilled with various emotions the dumb assembly,— "to Boabdil el Chico, king of Granada, Ferdinand of Arragon and Isabel of Castile send royal greeting. They command me to express their hope that the war is at length concluded, and they offer to the king of Granada such terms of capitulation as a king, without dishonour, may receive. In the stead of this city, which their Most Christian Majesties will restore to their own dominion, as is just, they offer, O king, princely territories in the Alpuxarras mountains to your sway, holding them by oath of fealty to the Spanish crown. To the people of Granada their Most Christian Majesties promise full protection of property, life, and faith, under a government by their own magistrates and according to their own laws, exemption from tribute for three years, and taxes thereafter, regulated by the custom and ratio of their present imposts. To such Moors as, discontented with these provisions, would abandon Granada, are promised free passage for themselves and their wealth. In return for these marks of their royal bounty, their Most Christian Majesties summon Granada to surrender (if no succour meanwhile arrive) within seventy days. And these offers are now solemnly recorded in the presence and through the mission of the noble and renowned knight, Gonzalvo of Cordova, deputed by their Most Christian Majesties from their new city of Santa Fé."

When the herald had concluded, Boabdil cast his eye over

his thronged and splendid court. No glance of fire met his own; amidst the silent crowd a resigned content was alone to be perceived: the proposals exceeded the hope of the besieged.

"And," asked Boabdil, with a deep-drawn sigh, "if we reject these offers?"

"Noble prince," said Gonzalvo, earnestly, "ask us not to wound thine ears with the alternative. Pause, and consider of our offers; and if thou doubtest, O brave king! mount the towers of thine Alhambra, survey our legions marshalled beneath thy walls, and turn thine eyes upon a brave people, defeated, not by human valour, but by famine and the inscrutable will of God."

"Your monarchs shall have our answer, gentle Christian, perchance ere nightfall. And you, Sir Knight, who hast delivered a message bitter for kings to hear, receive at least our thanks for such bearing as might best mitigate the import. Our vizier will bear to your apartment those tokens of remembrance that are yet left to the monarch of Granada to bestow."

"Muza," resumed the king, as the Spaniards left the presence, "thou hast heard all. What is the last counsel thou canst give thy sovereign?"

The fierce Moor had with difficulty waited this license to utter such sentiments as death only could banish from that unconquerable heart. He rose, descended from the couch, and standing a little below the king, and facing the motley throng of all of wise or brave yet left to Granada, thus spoke: —

"Why should we surrender? Two hundred thousand inhabitants are yet within our walls; of these, twenty thousand, at least, are Moors, who have hands and swords. Why should we surrender? Famine presses us, it is true; but hunger, that makes the lion more terrible, shall it make the man more base? Do ye despair? So be it! Despair in the valiant ought to have an irresistible force. Despair has made cowards brave: shall it sink the brave to cowards? Let us arouse the people; hitherto we have depended too much upon the nobles. Let us collect our whole force, and march upon this new city while the soldiers of Spain are employed in their new profession of architects and builders. Hear me, O God and prophet of the Moslem! hear one who never was forsworn! If, Moors of Granada, ye adopt my counsel, I cannot promise you victory, but I promise you never to live without it; I promise you at least your independence, — for the dead know no chains! If we cannot live, let us so die that we may leave to remotest ages a glory that shall be more durable than kingdoms. King of Granada, this is the counsel of Muza Ben Abil Gazan."

The prince ceased; but he, whose faintest word had once breathed fire into the dullest, had now poured out his spirit upon frigid and lifeless matter. No man answered, no man moved.

Boabdil alone, clinging to the shadow of hope, turned at last towards the audience.

"Warriors and sages!" he said, "as Muza's counsel is your king's desire, say but the word, and ere the hour-glass shed its last sand, the blast of our trumpet shall be ringing through the Vivarrambla."

"O king, fight not against the will of fate; God is great!" replied the chief of the alfaquis.

"Alas!" said Abdelmelic, "if the voice of Muza and your own fall thus coldly upon us, how can ye stir the breadless and heartless multitude?"

"Is such your general thought and your general will?" said Boabdil.

A universal murmur answered, "Yes!"

"Go, then, Abdelmelic," resumed the ill-starred king, "go with yon Spaniards to the Christian camp, and bring us back the best terms you can obtain. The crown has passed from the head of El Zogoybi; Fate sets her seal upon my brow. Unfortunate was the commencement of my reign, — unfortunate its end. Break up the divan."

The words of Boabdil moved and penetrated an audience never till then so alive to his gentle qualities, his learned wisdom, and his natural valour. Many flung themselves at his feet, with tears and sighs, and the crowd gathered round to touch the hem of his robe.

Muza gazed at them in deep disdain, with folded arms and heaving breast.

"Women, not men," he exclaimed, "ye weep as if ye had not blood still left to shed! Ye are reconciled to the loss of liberty, because ye are told ye shall lose nothing else. Fools and dupes! I see, from the spot where my spirit stands above you, the dark and dismal future to which ye are crawling on your knees, — bondage and rapine; the violence of lawless lust; the persecution of hostile faith; your gold wrung from you by torture; your national name rooted from the soil. Bear this, and remember me! Farewell, Boabdil! you I pity not; for your gardens have yet a poison, and your armories a sword. Farewell, nobles and santons of Granada! I quit my country while it is yet free."

Scarcely had he ceased, ere he had disappeared from the hall. It was as the parting genius of Granada!

CHAPTER IV.

THE ADVENTURE OF THE SOLITARY HORSEMAN.

It was a burning and sultry noon when, through a small valley skirted by rugged and precipitous hills, at the distance of several leagues from Granada, a horseman, in complete armour, wound his solitary way. His mail was black and unadorned, on his vizor waved no plume; but there was something in his carriage and mien, and the singular beauty of his coal-black steed, which appeared to indicate a higher rank than the absence of page and squire, and the plainness of his accoutrements, would have denoted to a careless eye. He rode very slowly; and his steed, with the license of a spoiled favourite, often halted lazily in his sultry path as a tuft of herbage or the bough of some overhanging tree offered its temptation. At length, as he thus paused, a noise was heard in a copse that clothed the descent of a steep mountain, and the horse started suddenly back, forcing the traveller from his revery. He looked mechanically upward, and beheld the figure of a man bounding through the trees with rapid and irregular steps. It was a form that suited well the silence and solitude of the spot, and might have passed for one of those stern recluses — half hermit, half soldier — who in the earlier Crusades fixed their wild homes amidst the sands and caves of Palestine. The stranger supported his steps by a long staff. His hair and beard hung long and matted over his broad shoulders. A rusted mail, once splendid with arabesque enrichments, protected his breast; but the loose gown — a sort of tartan which descended below the cuirass — was rent and tattered, and his feet were bare; in his girdle was a short curved cimeter, a knife or dagger, and a parchment roll clasped and bound with iron.

As the horseman gazed at this abrupt intruder on the solitude, his frame quivered with emotion; and raising himself to his full height, he called aloud, "Fiend or santon, — whatsoever thou art, — what seekest thou in these lonely places far from the king thy counsels deluded, and the city betrayed by thy false prophecies and unhallowed charms?"

"Ha!" cried Almamen, for it was indeed the Israelite, "by thy black charger and the tone of thy haughty voice I know the hero of Granada. Rather, Muza Ben Abil Gazan, why art thou absent from the last hold of the Moorish empire?"

"Dost thou pretend to read the future, and art thou blind to the present? Granada has capitulated to the Spaniard. Alone I have left a land of slaves, and shall seek, in our ancestral Africa, some spot where the footstep of the misbe-liever hath not trodden."

"The fate of one bigotry is, then, sealed," said Almamen, gloomily; "but that which succeeds it is yet more dark."

"Dog!" cried Muza, couching his lance; "what art thou that thus blasphemest?"

"A Jew," replied Almamen, in a voice of thunder, and drawing his cimeter, — "a despised and despising Jew! Ask you more? I am the son of a race of kings. I was the worst enemy of the Moors till I found the Nazarene more hateful than the Moslem; and then even Muza himself was not their more renowned champion. Come on, if thou wilt, man to man; I defy thee!"

"No, no," muttered Muza, sinking his lance; "thy mail is rusted with the blood of the Spaniard, and this arm cannot smite the slayer of the Christian. Part we in peace."

"Hold, prince!" said Almamen, in an altered voice; "is thy country the sole thing dear to thee? Has the smile of woman never stolen beneath thine armour? Has thy heart never beat for softer meetings than the encounter of a foe?"

"Am I human, and a Moor?" returned Muza. "For once you divine aright; and could thy spells bestow on these eyes but one more sight of the last treasure left to me on earth, I should be as credulous of thy sorcery as Boabdil."

"Thou lovest her still, then, this Leila?"

"Dark necromancer, hast thou read my secret, and knowest thou the name of my beloved one? Ah! let me believe thee indeed wise, and reveal to me the spot of earth which holds the delight of my soul! Yes," continued the Moor, with increased emotion, and throwing up his vizor, as if for air, — "yes; Allah forgive me! but when all was lost at Granada, I had still one consolation in leaving my fated birthplace, — I had license to search for Leila; I had the hope to secure to my wanderings in distant lands one to whose glance the eyes of the houris would be dim. But I waste words. Tell me where is Leila, and conduct me to her feet."

"Moslem, I will lead thee to her," answered Almamen, gazing on the prince with an expression of strange and fearful exultation in his dark eyes, — "I will lead thee to her; follow me. It is only yesternight that I learned the walls that confined her; and from that hour to this have I journeyed over mountain and desert, without rest or food."

"Yet what is she to thee?" asked Muza, suspiciously.

"Thou shalt learn full soon. Let us on."

So saying, Almamen sprang forward with a vigour which the excitement of his mind supplied to the exhaustion of his body. Muza wonderingly pushed on his charger, and endeavoured to draw his mysterious guide into conversation; but

Almamen scarcely heeded him. And when he broke from his gloomy silence, it was but in incoherent and brief exclamations, often in a tongue foreign to the ear of his companion. The hardy Moor, though steeled against the superstitions of his race, less by the philosophy of the learned than the contempt of the brave, felt an awe gather over him as he glanced, from the giant rocks and lonely valleys, to the unearthly aspect and glittering eyes of the reputed sorcerer; and more than once he muttered such verses of the Koran as were esteemed by his countrymen the counterspell to the machinations of the evil genii.

It might be an hour that they had thus journeyed together, when Almamen paused abruptly. "I am wearied," said he, faintly; "and though time presses, I fear that my strength will fail me."

"Mount, then, behind me," returned the Moor, after some natural hesitation. "Jew though thou art, I will brave the contamination for the sake of Leila."

"Moor," cried the Hebrew, fiercely, "the contamination would be mine. Things of yesterday, as thy Prophet and thy creed are, thou canst not sound the unfathomable loathing which each heart, faithful to the Ancient of Days, feels for such as thou and thine."

"Now, by the Kaaba," said Muza, and his brow became dark, "another such word, and the hoofs of my steed shall trample the breath of blasphemy from thy body!"

"I would defy thee to the death," answered Almamen, disdainfully; "but I reserve the bravest of the Moors to witness a deed worthy of the descendant of Jephtha. But hist! I hear hoofs."

Muza listened, and his sharp ear caught a distinct ring upon the hard and rocky soil. He turned round, and saw Almamen gliding away through the thick underwood, until the branches concealed his form. Presently a curve in the path brought in view a Spanish cavalier mounted on an Andalusian jennet. The horseman was gayly singing one of the popular ballads of the time; and as it related to the feats of the Spaniards against the Moors, Muza's haughty blood was

already stirred, and his mustache quivered on his lip. "I
will change the air," muttered the Moslem, grasping his lance,
when, as the thought crossed him, he beheld the Spaniard
suddenly reel in his saddle and fall prostrate on the ground.
In the same instant Almamen had darted from his hiding-
place, seized the steed of the cavalier, mounted, and ere Muza
recovered from his surprise, was by the side of the Moor.

"By what harm," said Muza, curbing his barb, "didst thou
fell the Spaniard? Seemingly without a blow."

"As David felled Goliath,— by the pebble and the sling,"
answered Almamen, carelessly. "Now, then, spur forward,
if thou art eager to see thy Leila."

The horsemen dashed over the body of the stunned and
insensible Spaniard. Tree and mountain glided by; gradually the valley vanished, and a thick forest loomed upon their
path. Still they made on, though the interlaced boughs and
the raggedness of the footing somewhat obstructed their way;
until, as the sun began slowly to decline, they entered a
broad and circular space round which trees of the eldest
growth spread their motionless and shadowy boughs. In the
midmost sward was a rude and antique stone, resembling the
altar of some barbarous and departed creed. Here Almamen
abruptly halted, and muttered inaudibly to himself.

"What moves thee, dark stranger?" said the Moor; "and
why dost thou mutter and gaze on space?"

Almamen answered not, but dismounted, hung his bridle to
a branch of a scathed and riven elm, and advanced alone into
the middle of the space. "Dread and prophetic power that
art within me!" said the Hebrew, aloud, "this, then, is the
spot that, by dream and vision, thou hast foretold me wherein
to consummate and record the vow that shall sever from the
spirit the last weakness of the flesh. Night after night hast
thou brought before mine eyes, in darkness and in slumber,
the solemn solitude that I now survey. Be it so; I am
prepared!"

Thus speaking, he retired for a few moments into the wood,
collected in his arms the dry leaves and withered branches
which cumbered the desolate clay, and placed the fuel upon

the altar. Then, turning to the east, and raising his hands on high, he exclaimed, "Lo! upon this altar, once worshipped, perchance, by the heathen savage, the last bold spirit of thy fallen and scattered race dedicates, O Ineffable One! that precious offering Thou didst demand from a sire of old. Accept the sacrifice!"

As the Hebrew ended his adjuration he drew a phial from his bosom and sprinkled a few drops upon the arid fuel. A pale blue flame suddenly leaped up; and as it lighted the haggard but earnest countenance of the Israelite, Muza felt his Moorish blood congeal in his veins, and shuddered, though he scarce knew why. Almamen with his dagger severed from his head one of his long locks, and cast it upon the flame. He watched it until it was consumed; and then, with a stifled cry, fell upon the earth in a dead swoon. The Moor hastened to raise him; he chafed his hands and temples; he unbuckled the vest upon his bosom; he forgot that his comrade was a sorcerer and a Jew, so much had the agony of that excitement moved his sympathy.

It was not till several minutes had elapsed that Almamen, with a deep-drawn sigh, recovered from his swoon. "Ah, beloved one, bride of my heart!" he murmured, "was it for this that thou didst commend to me the only pledge of our youthful love? Forgive me! I restore her to the earth untainted by the Gentile." He closed his eyes again, and a strong convulsion shook his frame. It passed; and he rose as a man from a fearful dream, composed, and almost as it were refreshed, by the terrors he had undergone. The last glimmer of the ghastly light was dying away upon that ancient altar, and a low wind crept sighing through the trees.

"Mount, prince," said Almamen, calmly, but averting his eyes from the altar; "we shall have no more delays."

"Wilt thou not explain thy incantation?" asked Muza; "or is it, as my reason tells me, but the mummery of a juggler?"

"Alas, alas!" answered Almamen, in a sad and altered tone, "thou wilt soon know all."

CHAPTER V.

THE SACRIFICE.

THE sun was now sinking slowly through those masses of
purple cloud which belong to Iberian skies, when, emerging
from the forest, the travellers saw before them a small and
lovely plain, cultivated like a garden.   Rows of orange and
citron trees were backed by the dark-green foliage of vines,
and these again found a barrier in girdling copses of chestnut,
oak, and the deeper verdure of pines; while, far to the horizon, rose the distant and dim outline of the mountain range,
scarcely distinguishable from the mellow colourings of the
heaven.   Through this charming spot went a slender and
sparkling torrent that collected its waters in a circular basin,
over which the rose and orange hung their contrasted blos-
soms.   On a gentle eminence above this plain, or garden,
rose the spires of a convent; and though it was still clear
daylight, the long and pointed lattices were illumined within,
and as the horsemen cast their eyes upon the pile, the sound
of the holy chorus — made more sweet and solemn from its
own indistinctness, from the quiet of the hour, from the sudden and sequestered loveliness of that spot, suiting so well
the ideal calm of the conventual life — rolled its music
through the odorous and lucent air.

But that scene and that sound, so calculated to soothe and
harmonize the thought, seemed to arouse Almamen into agony
and passion.   He smote his breast with his clenched hand,
and shrieking, rather than exclaiming, "God of my fathers!
have I come too late?" buried his spurs to the rowels in the
sides of his panting steed.   Along the sward, through the fragrant shrubs, athwart the pebbly and shallow torrent, up the
ascent to the convent, sped the Israelite.   Muza, wondering
and half reluctant, followed at a little distance.   Clearer and

nearer came the voices of the choir; broader and redder glowed the tapers from the Gothic casements. The porch of the convent chapel was reached; the Hebrew sprang from his horse. A small group of the peasants dependent on the convent loitered reverently round the threshold; pushing through them, as one frantic, Almamen entered the chapel and disappeared.

A minute elapsed. Muza was at the door, but the Moor paused irresolutely ere he dismounted. "What is the ceremony?" he asked of the peasants.

"A nun is about to take the vows," answered one of them.

A cry of alarm, of indignation, of terror, was heard within. Muza no longer delayed; he gave his steed to the bystander, pushed aside the heavy curtain that screened the threshold, and was within the chapel.

By the altar gathered a confused and disordered group, — the sisterhood, with their abbess. Round the consecrated rail flocked the spectators, breathless and amazed. Conspicuous above the rest, on the elevation of the holy place, stood Almamen with his drawn dagger in his right hand, his left arm clasped around the form of a novice, whose dress, not yet replaced by the serge, bespoke her the sister fated to the veil; and on the opposite side of that sister, one hand on her shoulder, the other rearing on high the sacred crucifix, stood a stern, commanding form, in the white robes of the Dominican order: it was Tomas de Torquemada.

"Avaunt, Abaddon!" were the first words which reached Muza's ear as he stood, unnoticed, in the middle of the aisle; "here thy sorcery and thine arts cannot avail thee. Release the devoted one of God!"

"She is mine! she is my daughter! I claim her from thee as a father, in the name of the great Sire of Man!"

"Seize the sorcerer, seize him!" exclaimed the Inquisitor, as, with a sudden movement, Almamen cleared his way through the scattered and dismayed group, and stood with his daughter in his arms on the first step of the consecrated platform.

But not a foot stirred, not a hand was raised. The epithet bestowed on the intruder had only breathed a supernatural terror into the audience; and they would have sooner rushed upon a tiger in his lair than on the lifted dagger and savage aspect of that grim stranger.

"Oh, my father," then said a low and faltering voice, that startled Muza as a voice from the grave, "wrestle not against the decrees of Heaven. Thy daughter is not compelled to her solemn choice. Humbly, but devotedly, a convert to the Christian creed, her only wish on earth is to take the conse· crated and eternal vow."

"Ha!" groaned the Hebrew, suddenly relaxing his hold, as his daughter fell on her knees before him, "then have I indeed been told, as I have foreseen, the worst. The veil is rent, the spirit hath left the temple. Thy beauty is desecrated; thy form is but unhallowed clay. Dog!" he cried more fiercely, glaring round upon the unmoved face of the Inquisitor, "this is thy work. But thou shalt not triumph. Here, by thine own shrine, I spit at and defy thee, as once before amidst the tortures of thy inhuman court. Thus — thus — thus — Almamen the Jew delivers the last of his house from the curse of Galilee!"

"Hold, murderer!" cried a voice of thunder; and an armed man burst through the crowd and stood upon the platform.

It was too late: thrice the blade of the Hebrew had passed through that innocent breast; thrice was it reddened with that virgin blood. Leila fell in the arms of her lover; her dim eyes rested upon his countenance as it shone upon her, beneath his lifted vizor; a faint and tender smile played upon her lips, — Leila was no more.

One hasty glance Almamen cast upon his victim, and then, with a wild laugh that woke every echo in the dreary aisles, he leaped from the place. Brandishing his bloody weapon above his head, he dashed through the coward crowd and ere even the startled Dominican had found a voice, the tramp of his headlong steed rang upon the air; an instant, and all was silent.

But over the murdered girl leaned the Moor, as yet incredulous of her death, her head, still unshorn of its purple tresses, pillowed on his lap, her icy hand clasped in his, and her blood weltering fast over his armour. None disturbed him; for, habited as the knights of Christendom, none suspected his faith, and all, even the Dominican, felt a thrill of sympathy at his distress. How he came hither, with what object, what hope, their thoughts were too much locked in pity to conjecture. There, voiceless and motionless, bent the Moor, until one of the monks approached and felt the pulse, to ascertain if life was, indeed, utterly gone.

The Moor at first waved him haughtily away; but when he divined the monk's purpose, suffered him in silence to take the beloved hand. He fixed on him his dark and imploring eyes; and when the father dropped the hand, and, gently shaking his head, turned away, a deep and agonizing groan was all that the audience heard from that heart in which the last iron of fate had entered. Passionately he kissed the brow, the cheeks, the lips of the hushed and angel face, and rose from the spot.

"What dost thou here, and what knowest thou of yon murderous enemy of God and man?" asked the Dominican, approaching.

Muza made no reply, as he stalked slowly through the chapel. The audience was touched to sudden tears. "Forbear!" said they, almost with one accord, to the harsh Inquisitor; "he hath no voice to answer thee."

And thus, amidst the oppressive grief and sympathy of the Christian throng, the unknown Paynim reached the door, mounted his steed, and as he turned once more and cast a hurried glance upon the fatal pile, the bystanders saw the large tears rolling down his swarthy cheeks.

Slowly that coal-black charger wound down the hillock, crossed the quiet and lovely garden, and vanished amidst the forest. And never was known, to Moor or Christian, the future fate of the hero of Granada. Whether he reached in safety the shores of his ancestral Africa and carved out new fortunes and a new name, or whether death, by disease or strife, terminated obscurely his glorious and brief career, mystery — deep and unpenetrated even by the fancies of the thousand bards who have consecrated his deeds — wraps in everlasting shadow the destinies of Muza Ben Abil Gazan from that hour when the setting sun threw its parting ray over his stately form and his ebon barb, disappearing amidst the breathless shadows of the forest.

CHAPTER VI.

THE RETURN, — THE RIOT, — THE TREACHERY, — AND THE DEATH.

It was the eve of the fatal day on which Granada was to be delivered to the Spaniards, and in that subterranean vault beneath the house of Almamen, before described, three elders of the Jewish persuasion were met.

"Trusty and well-beloved Ximen," cried one, a wealthy and usurious merchant, with a twinkling and humid eye, and a sleek and unctuous aspect, which did not, however, suffice to disguise something fierce and crafty in his low brow and pinched lips, — "trusty and well-beloved Ximen," said this Jew, "truly thou hast served us well, in yielding to thy persecuted brethren this secret shelter. Here, indeed, may the heathen search for us in vain! Verily, my veins grow warm again, and thy servant hungereth and hath thirst."

"Eat, Isaac, eat, — yonder are viands prepared for thee; eat, and spare not. And thou, Elias, wilt thou not draw near the board? The wine is old and precious, and will revive thee."

"Ashes and hyssop, hyssop and ashes, are food and drink for me," answered Elias, with passionate bitterness; "they have razed my house, they have burned my granaries, they have molten down my gold. I am a ruined man!"

"Nay," said Ximen, who gazed at him with a malevolent eye; for so utterly had years and sorrows mixed with gall even the one kindlier sympathy he possessed that he could not resist an inward chuckle over the very afflictions he relieved, and the very impotence he protected, — "nay, Elias, thou hast wealth yet left in the seaport towns sufficient to buy up half Granada."

"The Nazarene will seize it all," cried Elias; "I see it already in his grasp."

"Nay, thinkest thou so? And wherefore?" asked Ximen, startled into sincere, because selfish, anxiety.

"Mark me. Under license of the truce, I went, last night, to the Christian camp; I had an interview with the Christian king; and when he heard my name and faith, his very beard curled with ire. 'Hound of Belial!' he roared forth, 'has not thy comrade carrion, the sorcerer Almamen, sufficiently deceived and insulted the majesty of Spain? For his sake ye shall have no quarter. Tarry here another instant, and thy corpse shall be swinging to the winds! Go, and count over thy misgotten wealth: just census shall be taken of it; and if thou defraudest our holy impost by one piece of copper, thou shalt sup with Dives!' Such was my mission and mine answer. I return home to see the ashes of mine house. Woe is me!"

"And this we owe to Almamen, the pretended Jew!" cried Isaac from his solitary, but not idle, place at the board.

"I would this knife were at his false throat!" growled Elias, clutching his poniard with his long, bony fingers.

"No chance of that," muttered Ximen; "he will return no more to Granada. The vulture and the worm have divided his carcass between them ere this; and," he added, inly with a hideous smile, "his house and his gold have fallen into the hands of old, childless Ximen!"

"This is a strange and fearful vault," said Isaac, quaffing a large goblet of the hot wine of the Vega; "here might the Witch of Endor have raised the dead. Yon door, — whither doth it lead?"

"Through passages none that I know of, save my master, hath trodden," answered Ximen. "I have heard that they reach even to the Alhambra. Come, worthy Elias, thy form trembles with the cold; take this wine."

"Hist!" said Elias, shaking from limb to limb; "our pur-suers are upon us, — I hear a step!"

As he spoke, the door to which Isaac had pointed, slowly opened, and Almamen entered the vault.

Had, indeed, a new Witch of Endor conjured up the dead, the apparition would not more have startled and appalled that goodly trio. Elias, griping his knife, retreated to the farthest end of the vault. Isaac dropped the goblet he was about to drain, and fell upon his knees. Ximen alone, growing, if possible, a shade more ghastly, retained something of self-possession as he muttered to himself: "He lives, and his gold is not mine! Curse him!"

Seemingly unconscious of the strange guests his sanctuary shrouded, Almamen stalked on, like a man walking in his sleep.

Ximen roused himself, softly unbarred the door which admitted to the upper apartments, and motioned to his comrades to avail themselves of the opening; but as Isaac, the first to accept the hint, crept across, Almamen fixed upon him his terrible eye, and appearing suddenly to awake to consciousness, shouted out, "Thou miscreant, Ximen, whom hast thou admitted to the secrets of thy lord? Close the door; these men must die!"

"Mighty master," said Ximen, calmly, "is thy servant to blame that he believed the rumour that declared thy death? These men are of our holy faith whom I have snatched from the violence of the sacrilegious and maddened mob. No spot but this seemed safe from the popular frenzy."

"Are ye Jews?" said Almamen. "Ah, yes! I know ye now,— things of the market-place and bazaar! Oh, ye are Jews indeed! Go, go! Leave me!"

Waiting no further license, the three vanished; but ere he quitted the vault, Elias turned back his scowling countenance on Almamen (who had sunk again into an absorbed meditation) with a glance of vindictive ire. Almamen was alone.

In less than a quarter of an hour Ximen returned to seek his master, but the place was again deserted.

It was midnight in the streets of Granada, — midnight, but not repose. The multitude, roused into one of their paroxysms of wrath and sorrow by the reflection that the morrow was indeed the day of their subjection to the Christian foe, poured forth through the streets to the number of twenty thousand. It was a wild and stormy night; those formidable gusts of wind, which sometimes sweep in sudden winter from the snows of the Sierra Nevada, howled through the tossing groves and along the winding streets. But the tempest seemed to heighten, as if by the sympathy of the elements, the popular storm and whirlwind. Brandishing arms and torches, and gaunt with hunger, the dark forms of the frantic Moors seemed like ghouls or spectres, rather than mortal men, as, apparently without an object save that of venting their own disquietude or exciting the fears of earth, they swept through the desolate city.

In the broad space of the Vivarrambla the crowd halted, irresolute in all else, but resolved at least that something for Granada should yet be done. They were for the most armed in their Moorish fashion; but they were wholly without leaders, — not a noble, a magistrate, an officer, would have dreamed of the hopeless enterprise of violating the truce with Ferdinand. It was a mere popular tumult, — the madness of a mob; but not the less formidable, for it was an Eastern mob, and a mob with sword and shaft, with buckler and mail, — the mob by which Oriental empires have been built and overthrown! There, in the splendid space that had witnessed the games and tournaments of that Arab and African chivalry, — there, where for many a lustrum kings had reviewed devoted and conquering armies, assembled those desperate men, the loud winds agitating their tossing torches that struggled against the moonless night.

"Let us storm the Alhambra!" cried one of the band; "let us seize Boabdil, and place him in the midst of us; let us rush against the Christians, buried in their proud repose!"

"Lelilies, Lelilies! The Keys and the Crescent!" shouted the mob.

The shout died, and at the verge of the space was suddenly heard a once familiar and ever-thrilling voice.

The Moors who heard it turned round in amaze and awe, and beheld, raised upon the stone upon which the criers or heralds had been wont to utter the royal proclamations, the form of Almamen the santon, whom they had deemed already with the dead.

"Moors and people of Granada!" he said, in a solemn but hollow voice, "I am with you still. Your monarch and your heroes have deserted you, but I am with you to the last! Go not to the Alhambra; the fort is impenetrable, the guard faithful. Night will be wasted, and day bring upon you the Christian army. March to the gates; pour along the Vega; descend at once upon the foe!"

He spoke, and drew forth his sabre, — it gleamed in the torchlight; the Moors bowed their head in fanatic reverence; the santon sprang from the stone, and passed into the centre of the crowd.

Then once more arose joyful shouts. The multitude had found a leader worthy of their enthusiasm, and in regular order they formed themselves rapidly, and swept down the narrow streets.

Swelled by several scattered groups of desultory marauders (the ruffians and refuse of the city), the infidel numbers were now but a few furlongs from the great gate whence they had been wont to issue on the foe. And then, perhaps, had the Moors passed these gates and reached the Christian encampment, lulled, as it was, in security and sleep, that wild army of twenty thousand desperate men might have saved Granada, and Spain might at this day possess the only civilized empire which the faith of Mohammed ever founded.

But the evil star of Boabdil prevailed. The news of the insurrection in the city reached him. Two aged men from the lower city arrived at the Alhambra, demanded and obtained an audience; and the effect of that interview was instantaneous upon Boabdil. In the popular frenzy he saw only a justifiable excuse for the Christian king to break the conditions of the treaty, raze the city, and exterminate the inhabitants. Touched by a generous compassion for his subjects, and actuated no less by a high sense of kingly honour, which led him to preserve a truce solemnly sworn to, he once more mounted his cream-coloured charger, with the two elders

who had sought him by his side, and at the head of his guard
rode from the Alhambra. The sound of his trumpets, the
tramp of his steeds, the voice of his heralds, simultaneously
reached the multitude, and ere they had leisure to decide their
course, the king was in the midst of them.

"What madness is this, O my people?" cried Boabdil, spur-
ring into the midst of the throng,— "whither would ye go?"

"Against the Christian! against the Goth!" shouted a
thousand voices. "Lead us on! The santon is risen from
the dead, and will ride by thy right hand!"

"Alas!" resumed the king, "ye would march against the
Christian king! Remember that our hostages are in his
power; remember that he will desire no better excuse to
level Granada with the dust, and put you and your children
to the sword. We have made such treaty as never yet was
made between foe and foe. Your lives, laws, wealth, — all
are saved. Nothing is lost, save the crown of Boabdil. I
am the only sufferer. So be it. My evil star brought on you
these evil destinies; without me, you may revive, and be once
more a nation. Yield to fate to-day, and you may grasp her
proudest awards to-morrow. To succumb is not to be subdued. But go forth against the Christians, and if you win one
battle, it is but to incur a more terrible war; if you lose, it
is not honourable capitulation, but certain extermination, to
which you rush! Be persuaded, and listen once again to your
king."

The crowd were moved, were softened, were half-convinced.
They turned in silence towards their santon; and Almamen
did not shrink from the appeal, but stood forth, confronting
the king.

"King of Granada," he cried aloud, "behold thy friend,
thy prophet! Lo, I assure you victory!"

"Hold!" interrupted Boabdil; "thou hast deceived and
betrayed me too long. Moors, know ye this pretended santon? He is of no Moslem creed. He is a hound of Israel
who would sell you to the best bidder. Slay him!"

"Ha!" cried Almamen, "and who is my accuser?"

"Thy servant, — behold him!" At these words the royal

guards lifted their torches, and the glare fell redly on the death-like features of Ximen.

"Light of the world, there be other Jews that know him," said the traitor.

"Will ye suffer a Jew to lead you, O race of the prophet?" cried the king.

The crowd stood confused and bewildered. Almamen felt his hour was come; he remained silent, his arms folded, his brow erect.

"Be there any of the tribes of Moisa amongst the crowd?" cried Boabdil, pursuing his advantage. "If so, let them approach and testify what they know." Forth came, not from the crowd, but from amongst Boabdil's train, a well-known Israelite.

"We disown this man of blood and fraud," said Elias, bowing to the earth; "but he was of our creed."

"Speak, false santon, art thou dumb?" cried the king.

"A curse light on thee, dull fool!" cried Almamen, fiercely. "What matters who the instrument that would have restored to thee thy throne? Yes! I, who have ruled thy councils, who have led thine armies, I am of the race of Joshua and of Samuel, — and the Lord of Hosts is the God of Almamen!"

A shudder ran through that mighty multitude; but the looks, the mien, and the voice of the man awed them, and not a weapon was raised against him. He might, even then, have passed scathless through the crowd; he might have borne to other climes his burning passions and his torturing woes: but his care for life was past; he desired but to curse his dupes, and to die. He paused, looked round, and burst into a laugh of such bitter and haughty scorn as the tempted of earth may hear in the halls below from the lips of Eblis.

"Yes," he exclaimed, "such I am! I have been your idol and your lord. I may be your victim, but in death I am your vanquisher. Christian and Moslem alike my foe, I would have trampled upon both. But the Christian, wiser than you, gave me smooth words, and I would have sold you to his power; wickeder than you, he deceived me, and I would have crushed him, that I might have continued to deceive and rule

the puppets that ye call your chiefs. But they for whom I
toiled and laboured and sinned; for whom I surrendered peace
and ease, yea, and a daughter's person and a daughter's blood,
—they have betrayed me to your hands, and the Curse of Old
rests with them evermore. Amen! The disguise is rent;
Almamen the santon is the son of Issachar the Jew!"

More might he have said, but the spell was broken. With
a ferocious yell those living waves of the multitude rushed
over the stern fanatic. Six cimeters passed through him, and
he fell not; at the seventh he was a corpse. Trodden in the
clay, then whirled aloft, limb torn from limb, — ere a man
could have drawn breath nine times, scarce a vestige of the
human form was left to the mangled and bloody clay.

One victim sufficed to slake the wrath of the crowd. They
gathered like wild beasts whose hunger is appeased, around
their monarch, who in vain had endeavoured to stay their
summary revenge, and who now, pale and breathless, shrank
from the passions he had excited. He faltered forth a few
words of remonstrance and exhortation, turned the head of
his steed, and took his way to his palace.

The crowd dispersed, but not yet to their homes. The
crime of Almamen worked against his whole race. Some
rushed to the Jews' quarter, which they set on fire; others to
the lonely mansion of Almamen.

Ximen on quitting the king had been before the mob. Not
anticipating such an effect of the popular rage, he had hastened to the house, which he now deemed at length his own.
He had just reached the treasury of his dead lord, he had just
feasted his eyes on the massive ingots and glittering gems; in
the lust of his heart he had just cried aloud, "And these are
mine!"—when he heard the roar of the mob below the wall,
when he saw the glare of their torches against the casement.
It was in vain that he shrieked aloud, "I am the man that
exposed the Jew!" the wild winds scattered his words over a
deafened audience. Driven from his chamber by the smoke
and flame, afraid to venture forth amongst the crowd, the miser
loaded himself with the most precious of the store; he descended the steps, he bent his way to the secret vault, when

suddenly the floor, pierced by the flames, crashed under him, and the fire rushed up in a fiercer and more rapid volume as the death-shriek broke through that lurid shroud.

Such were the principal events of the last night of the Moorish dynasty in Granada.

CHAPTER VII.

THE END.

DAY dawned upon Granada; the populace had sought their homes, and a profound quiet wrapped the streets, save where, from the fires committed in the late tumult, was yet heard the crash of roofs or the crackle of the light and fragrant timber employed in those pavilions of the summer. The manner in which the mansions of Granada were built, each separated from the other by extensive gardens, fortunately prevented the flames from extending. But the inhabitants cared so little for the hazard that not a single guard remained to watch the result. Now and then some miserable forms in the Jewish gown might be seen cowering by the ruins of their house, like the souls that, according to Plato, watch in charnels over their own mouldering bodies. Day dawned, and the beams of the winter sun, smiling away the clouds of the past night, played cheerily on the murmuring waves of the Xenil and the Darro.

Alone upon a balcony commanding that stately landscape stood the last of the Moorish kings. He had sought to bring to his aid all the lessons of the philosophy he had cultivated.

"What are we," thought the musing prince, "that we should fill the world with ourselves, we kings! Earth resounds with the crash of my falling throne; on the ear of races unborn the echo will live prolonged. But what have I lost? Nothing that was necessary to my happiness, my repose, — nothing save the source of all my wretchedness, the Marah of my life! Shall I less enjoy heaven and earth, or thought or action, or man's more material luxuries of food or sleep, — the common and the cheap desires of all? Arouse thee, then, O heart within me! Many and deep emotions of sorrow or of joy are yet left to break the monotony of existence."

He paused, and at the distance his eye fell upon the lonely minarets of the distant and deserted palace of Muza Ben Abil Gazan.

"Thou wert right, then," resumed the king, — "thou wert right, brave spirit, not to pity Boabdil. But not because death was in his power; man's soul is greater than his fortunes, and there is majesty in a life that towers above the ruins that fall around its path."

He turned away, and his cheek suddenly grew pale, for he heard, in the courts below, the tread of hoofs, the bustle of preparation: it was the hour for his departure. His philosophy vanished; he groaned aloud, and re-entered the chamber just as his vizier and the chief of his guard broke upon his solitude.

The old vizier attempted to speak, but his voice failed him.

"It is time, then, to depart," said Boabdil, with calmness; "let it be so: render up the palace and the fortress, and join thy friend, no more thy monarch, in his new home."

He stayed not for reply; he hurried on, descended to the court, flung himself on his barb, and with a small and saddened train passed through the gate which we yet survey, by a blackened and crumbling tower overgrown with vines and ivy; thence amidst gardens now appertaining to the convent of the victor faith, he took his mournful and unwitnessed way. When he came to the middle of the hill that rises above those gardens, the steel of the Spanish armour gleamed upon him as the detachment sent to occupy the palace marched over the summit in steady order and profound silence.

At the head of this vanguard rode, upon a snow-white palfrey, the Bishop of Avila, followed by a long train of barefooted monks. They halted as Boabdil approached, and the grave bishop saluted him with the air of one who addresses an infidel and an inferior. With the quick sense of dignity

common to the great, and yet more to the fallen, Boabdil felt,
but resented not, the pride of the ecclesiastic. "Go, Christian," said he, mildly, "the gates of the Alhambra are open,
and Allah has bestowed the palace and the city upon your
king. May his virtues atone the faults of Boabdil!" So
saying, and waiting no answer, he rode on, without looking
to the right or left. The Spaniards also pursued their way.
The sun had fairly risen above the mountains when Boabdil
and his train beheld, from the eminence on which they were,
the whole armament of Spain; and at the same moment,
louder than the tramp of horse or the flash of arms, was
heard distinctly the solemn chant of *Te Deum*, which pre-
ceded the blaze of the unfurled and lofty standards. Boabdil,
himself still silent, heard the groans and exclamations of his
train; he turned to cheer or chide them, and then saw from
his own watch-tower, with the sun shining full upon its pure
and dazzling surface, the silver cross of Spain. His Alhambra was already in the hands of the foe, while beside that
badge of the holy war waved the gay and flaunting flag of
Saint Iago, the canonized Mars of the chivalry of Spain.

At that sight the king's voice died within him; he gave the
rein to his barb, impatient to close the fatal ceremonial, and
did not slacken his speed till almost within bowshot of the
first ranks of the army. Never had Christian war assumed
a more splendid or imposing aspect. Far as the eye could
reach extended the glittering and gorgeous lines of that goodly
power, bristling with sunlit spears and blazoned banners;
while beside murmured and glowed and danced, the silver
and laughing Xenil, careless what lord should possess, for
his little day, the banks that bloomed by its everlasting
course. By a small mosque halted the flower of the army.
Surrounded by the arch-priests of that mighty hierarchy, the
peers and princes of a court that rivalled the Rolands of
Charlemagne, was seen the kingly form of Ferdinand himself, with Isabel at his right hand, and the high-born dames
of Spain, relieving, with their gay colours and sparkling
gems, the sterner splendour of the crested helmet and pol-
ished mail.

Within sight of the royal group Boabdil halted, composed his aspect so as best to conceal his soul, and, a little in advance of his scanty train, but never, in mien and majesty, more a king, the son of Abdallah met his haughty conqueror.

At the sight of his princely countenance and golden hair, his comely and commanding beauty, made more touching by youth, a thrill of compassionate admiration ran through that assembly of the brave and fair. Ferdinand and Isabel slowly advanced to meet their late rival, — their new subject; and as Boabdil would have dismounted, the Spanish king placed his hand upon his shoulder. "Brother and prince," said he, "forget thy sorrows; and may our friendship hereafter console thee for reverses against which thou hast contended as a hero and a king, — resisting man, but resigned at length to God!"

Boabdil did not affect to return this bitter, but unintentional, mockery of compliment. He bowed his head, and remained a moment silent; then, motioning to his train, four of his officers approached, and kneeling beside Ferdinand, proffered to him upon a silver buckler the keys of the city.

"O king," then said Boabdil, "accept the keys of the last hold which has resisted the arms of Spain! The empire of the Moslem is no more. Thine are the city and the people of Granada; yielding to thy prowess, they yet confide in thy mercy."

"They do well," said the king; "our promises shall not be broken. But since we know the gallantry of Moorish cavaliers, not to us, but to gentler hands, shall the keys of Granada be surrendered."

Thus saying, Ferdinand gave the keys to Isabel, who would have addressed some soothing flatteries to Boabdil. But the emotion and excitement were too much for her compassionate heart, heroine and queen though she was; and when she lifted her eyes upon the calm and pale features of the fallen monarch, the tears gushed from them irresistibly, and her voice died in murmurs. A faint flush overspread the features of Boabdil, and there was a momentary pause of embarrassment which the Moor was the first to break.

"Fair queen," said he, with mournful and pathetic dignity, "thou canst read the heart that thy generous sympathy touches and subdues: this is thy last, nor least glorious, conquest. But I detain you; let not my aspect cloud your triumph. Suffer me to say farewell."

"May we not hint at the blessed possibility of conversion?" whispered the pious queen through her tears to her royal consort.

"Not now, not now, by Saint Iago!" returned Ferdinand, quickly, and in the same tone, willing himself to conclude a painful conference. He then added aloud: "Go, my brother, and fair fortune with you! Forget the past."

Boabdil smiled bitterly, saluted the royal pair with profound and silent reverence, and rode slowly on, leaving the army below, as he ascended the path that led to his new principality beyond the Alpuxarras. As the trees snatched the Moorish cavalcade from the view of the king, Ferdinand ordered the army to recommence its march; and trumpet and cymbal presently sent their music to the ear of the Moslems.

Boabdil spurred on at full speed till his panting charger halted at the little village where his mother, his slaves, and his faithful Amine (sent on before) awaited him. Joining these, he proceeded without delay upon his melancholy path.

They ascended that eminence which is the pass into the Alpuxarras. From its height, the vale, the rivers, the spires, the towers of Granada broke gloriously upon the view of the little band. They halted mechanically and abruptly; every eye was turned to the beloved scene. The proud shame of baffled warriors, the tender memories of home, of childhood, of fatherland, swelled every heart and gushed from every eye. Suddenly the distant boom of artillery broke from the citadel, and rolled along the sunlit valley and crystal river. A universal wail burst from the exiles; it smote, it overpowered the heart of the ill-starred king, in vain seeking to wrap himself in Eastern pride or Stoical philosophy. The tears gushed from his eyes, and he covered his face with his hands.

Then said his haughty mother, gazing at him with hard and disdainful eyes, in that unjust and memorable reproach which history has preserved: "Ay, weep like a woman over what thou couldst not defend like a man!"

Boabdil raised his countenance with indignant majesty, when he felt his hand tenderly clasped, and, turning round, saw Amine by his side.

"Heed her not, heed her not, Boabdil!" said the slave; "never didst thou seem to me more noble than in that sorrow. Thou wert a hero for thy throne, but feel still, O light of mine eyes, a woman for thy people!"

"God is great," said Boabdil, "and God comforts me still! Thy lips, which never flattered me in my power, have no reproach for me in my affliction!"

He said, and smiled upon Amine: it was *her* hour of triumph.

The band wound slowly on through the solitary defiles; and that place where the king wept, and the woman soothed, is still called "El ultimo suspiro del Moro," — THE LAST SIGH OF THE MOOR!

THE END.